Shadows of Deception
Unearthing the Dark Side of Desire
by Ron Milione

INDEX/ TABLE OF CONTENTS

Presentation

Whispers in the Dark

The Allure of Sin

A Society of Lies

Broken Portraits

Trust on the Brink

Twisted Loyalties

Nightshade

Revelations Through the Veil

The Hour of Reckoning

Faces of the Dark

Concluding: Thank You for Joining the Adventure!

Hey there, fellow adventurer!

Welcome to a world bursting with imagination and wonder! This book is not just a collection of pages; it's a portal to an extraordinary place that was dreamt up during countless nights of inspired brainstorming and passionate research. The idea started to bubble up in my mind after I stumbled upon an old, dusty tome in a second-hand bookstore. Its pages were yellowed with age, yet the stories within them ignited a fire in my soul. I found myself lost in thought about the worlds we create in our minds and how those worlds can inspire us to live fuller, bolder lives.

Along the way, I dove deep into a rabbit hole of research—pouring over texts, interviewing experts, and even embarking on spontaneous field trips. Each detail added a layer to this intricate tapestry I wanted to weave for you. Yes, you read that right! Every sentence, every character, every twist and turn in this book has been crafted with you in mind, dear reader. I want you to feel that rush, that exhilaration that comes with each page turn.

I also had the privilege of collaborating with a remarkable group of believers—artists, fellow writers, and the most enthusiastic beta readers who dared to take my wild ideas and run with them. Their insights were priceless, helping me refine this masterpiece into something vibrant and alive. I'm thrilled to share it all with you. Prepare yourself for a rollercoaster of emotions, from laughter to tears and everything in between.

This book is both a reflection of my journey and an invitation for you to partake in an adventure unlike any other. I encourage you to savor every word, every chapter, and allow yourself to slip into the world we've created. You'll laugh, you'll cry, and you might even find pieces of yourself scattered throughout the narrative.

My hope is that by the time you reach the last page, you'll feel like you've journeyed alongside me, that this tale has resonated with your life in ways I can only dream of.

So dig in! I promise you it will be worth it. Remember to keep an open heart and a curious mind as you travel through this land of creativity. Let the world seep into your very bones and inspire you to dream bigger, to live more vividly, and to embrace the magic that life offers each and every day.

Thank you for joining me on this journey, and I genuinely hope it awakens something profound within you. Get ready to embark on this adventure, where anything is possible, and your imagination is your only limit. Trust in the magic of storytelling, and let it lead you to places you never knew existed.

Here's to the adventure that awaits—hold on tight and let us dive in together!

In joyful anticipation,

Ron Milione

All rights to this book are reserved. No permission is given for any part of this book to be reproduced, transmitted in any form, or means; electronic or mechanical, stored in a retrieval system, photocopied, recorded, scanned, or otherwise. Any of these actions require the proper written permission of the author.

DISCLAIMER

The information provided within this book is for general information and for research and educational purposes only. The author makes no representations or warranties, express or implied, about the completeness, accuracy, reliability, suitability, or availability with respect to the information, products, services, or related graphics contained in this book for any purpose. Any use of this information is at your own risk.

Printed by AMAZON Worldwide Publication

Printed in the United States of America

Also available at AMAZON Book Stores
Welcome Summer 2025

First Printing Edition, 2025

ISBN: 9798282723311

This book is dedicated to my lovely wife Lynne,

and my best little companion, Bandit the POM!

Whispers in the Dark

The City Awakens

Elena Rourke took a deep breath, inhaling the damp, earthy scent of the cobblestones that twisted beneath her feet. The air hung heavy with the remnants of rain, soaking into the cracks of the pavement and mingling with the muffled sounds of the city awakening to the night. Each step brought a crisp crackle of dried leaves, remnants of autumn clinging to life in the shadows, and as her flashlight beam sliced through the darkness, it illuminated not just the way ahead but the pulsating secrets hidden beneath the surface of the city.

A distant siren wailed, echoing off the scarred brick walls surrounding her, underscoring the tension buried within the veins of the city. Elena kept her eyes peeled, determined to sift through the chaos of urban life that thrived under the cloak of darkness. Each flicker of her flashlight brought to light forgotten tales and whispered truths, stories lost in the din of revelry, a soundtrack familiar to the night crawlers who animated the streets.

Tonight felt particularly charged. Perhaps it was the nipping wind that prickled her skin or the faint hum of electricity crackling in the air, but she could feel the city was alive. The shadows seemed to dance with laughter and whispered promises, masking something more sinister. All around her, the alleys were alive, tales of the missing socialite weaving in and out like the smoke from the cigarette of an unseen onlooker.

The soft light flickered across a mural, its colors faded yet alive, depicting a figure engulfed in shadow—an artist's vision of despair framed against the city backdrop. Elena paused for a moment, allowing herself to get lost in the beauty of the grim imagery. It beckoned to her, echoing the turbulent art of the tortured souls she often encountered. She was here to find answers, yet she was also here to explore the depth of sorrow that seeped from the city, as relentless as the rain that had just ceased.

She continued deeper into the heart of the maze-like streets, her flashlight an extension of her resolve. The murmurs of vagabonds spilled from the shadows, their fragmented narratives enticing yet cautioning. Her thoughts swirled with the conflicting emotions surrounding her investigation, memories of the glamorous yet troublesome socialite drifting through her mind like drifting petals from a once-lively bloom.

In the first alley, she encountered a figure hunched over, rummaging through a makeshift cart. "Can you spare some change?" the woman croaked, her voice a raspy whisper that blended with the wind. Elena frowned, considering the woman's tattered clothing, the hint of a scarf wrapping around her neck barely sufficient against the biting cold.

"I can't help you with money, but I need something of value—information. I'm looking for Marya Langston," Elena replied, attempting to keep her voice steady.

The woman's eyes narrowed, suspicion mingling with curiosity. "Marya, you say? Pretty little thing, she was. Danced among the stars above. Got snatched too close to the fire, if you ask me. You better watch for those with eyes that glimmer too bright—they don't have your best interests at heart."

Elena leaned closer, intrigued by the cryptic warning. "What do you mean by that? Who would want to hurt her?"

"Vultures circle when the sun sets, honey. You need to know that," she warned, her gaze darting, wary of eavesdroppers. "She had lovers aplenty, and each was thirsty for a taste of her fortune. But it was a dangerous game, tickling the fancies of wolves in sheep's clothing. You don't want to play that hand, sweetie. Better get clean away while you still can."

The vagabond's words echoed in the cavernous alley as Elena stepped back, taking in the depth of the city's nightshade grasp. "Thanks for the warning," she muttered, turning away, aware that with each piece of the puzzle, the shadows grew darker.

Elena made her way onward, the softer whispers of the evening beginning to coalesce into a clearer picture of tragedy. As the flashlight beam flickered down another alley, she turned the corner and was met with a scene bathed in dim light. A group of men gathered, their laughter raucous, rough-edged, sending her senses on high alert. Doubt gnawed at her, but the need for information drove her forward.

She approached the gathering cautiously. "You gentlemen heard of Marya Langston?" Elena called out, trying to maintain an air of authority.

One of the men, his hair slicked back and eyes glinting with mischief, turned to her, tilting his head. "And what's a nice lady like you doing in a place like this?" His voice was smooth, the kind that oozed charm and danger in equal measure.

"Marya, huh? We can talk about her. But these streets aren't free, you know. You got something to offer?"

Elena's brow furrowed; she hated this part of the job. The game of give and take could fracture, especially when the stakes rose high. "I can give you information in return for your stories," she replied firmly, not backing down from the challenge of trying to engage.

Another man, sitting against the wall with a cigarette dangling from his fingers, chimed in. "Marya liked to play in places where her beauty was a ticket, but she was never one to stick around when the party got dull. Might've outrun someone after all."

"Outrun?" Elena queried, her footsteps edging closer as their words led her deeper into the mystery.

The first man shrugged. "Heard she was seen with some shady characters. Rich boys playing hide-and-seek with reality while they drank their worries away. They say her mouth was as soft as her heart—pretty, but packed with secrets. Maybe she found out too much for her own good."

Elena raised an eyebrow. "So you're not surprised she's missing?"

The men shared a knowing look filled with unspoken truths, laughter dying down. "Life's cheap in this city. The pretty ones, they always draw the wrong kind of attention. Wouldn't be the first time a beauty vanished into the muck. You sure you want to dig deeper, lady?"

Elena felt the night's chill creep down her spine, but fear only solidified her resolve.

"I didn't come this far to turn back now," she said defiantly, forcing the confidence she felt waver even as she spoke.

The twisted path of her search promised dark roads ahead, but the murmurings of the night pressed on her mind like a gentle nudge—a reminder that the truth was often dangling just out of reach, much like the last flicker of light before complete darkness took hold.

As she made her way further into the city's labyrinthine layout, another alley called to her, dimly lit by a solitary street lamp, its presence a rare beacon in an otherwise darkened landscape. She stepped cautiously, absorbing the ambiance—the scent of damp earth mingling with smoke—when she spotted a rickety table housing a couple of disheveled patrons.

One of them, an older man with jagged scars etched across his face, leaned forward, eyes gleaming with a fiery recklessness. "You looking for trouble, lady? Or are you just another lost soul wandering these cursed paths?"

"Neither, actually. Just information. I'm looking for Marya Langston," Elena said, not afraid to sound vulnerable yet resolute.

The man froze, glancing sideways at the fellow seated beside him, who appeared similarly intrigued. "Why does everyone want to find her? She was a star shining too bright in these shadows. Perhaps it was better that she faded away before the night swallowed her whole."

Elena felt her heart quicken. "What do you mean?"

"Good intentions, all, that Marya had. But the city has a way of turning good into bad. It swallows trust like a ravenous beast.

You'll find no answers if you go searching too close to the flame, miss; too many will get burned."

She hesitated. "But there must be something you know. Tell me, please."

The old man leaned back, uncertainty brewing in his eyes. "It won't come without a price, lass."

Elena crossed her arms, sensing the stakes rise with her own urgency. "Then consider it an investment in the truth. The police won't dig into layers that I can. What did you hear?"

The man studied her for a beat longer, brow furrowed, perhaps measuring her motives. Eventually, he spoke, words weighted with significance. "She was tangled with someone powerful—money and desperation danced in tandem. They say he has connections that reach deeper than shadows. Hard to tell who's safer: her or the ones drawn to her light."

Elena felt her heart race again, the thrilling rush of the chase igniting her spirit. Beneath the unseemly facade of the city, a web of intrigue strung itself before her, each glimmer of insight leading her deeper into murky depths.

"Who is he?" she pressed, determination mingling with excitement.

The old man paused, glancing around the alley as if to ensure they weren't overheard. Then, in a conspiratorial hush, he uttered a name that sent a shiver through her—a name tangled with wealth, power, and a reputation drenched in darkness.

As the street lamp flickered faintly above her, maintaining the duality of light and shadow, decisions lay heavy on Elena's mind, cloaking her with uncertainty and apprehension. A name echoed through her thoughts that night, the quest illuminating the shadows and heightening the pulse of the missing socialite's story that remained crucial to unraveling the city's deepest secrets.

She tucked the new revelation in her pocket as she readied herself to leave the alley. The evening air was thick with anticipation, her resolve crystalizing into determination. She turned, stepping back into the bustling core of the city, her path forged not just by mystery but the haunting yet intoxicating echoes ringing through the night.

Each twist and turn of stone, each crooked smile from a stranger became a brushstroke in the unfolding portrait of Marya Langston—a life nestled within the darkness, a ticking clock against the skyline of neon lights arching above.

With a hand steadying her flashlight, the city awoke before her, a living entity poised to divulge its secrets, and Elena would not rest until its heart laid bare.

A Thread of Rumors

The door creaked open as Elena stepped into the dimly lit bar, the heavy scent of whiskey and despair engulfing her like a shroud. With each inhale, she could taste the history that clung to the wooden beams, the damp air thick with the echoes of countless stories, some whispered in confidence, others lost to the night. The flickering neon sign outside painted the room in shades of blue and red, casting eerie shadows against the faces of those seeking refuge from a world that had long forgotten them.

She made her way to the bar, the floor sticky beneath her heels, each step a reminder of the city's ghosts. The bartender, a grizzled veteran with a face etched by time and hardship, looked her way, his eyes narrowing as if sizing her up. Elena felt the weight of his gaze, a judgment that cut deeper than any words ever could.

"I'm looking for information," she said, keeping her voice steady, though the flicker of uncertainty threatened to crack her facade.

The bartender grunted, pouring a drink for a customer who looked as if he hadn't tasted anything but gin in weeks. "Information ain't cheap, lady." His voice was gravelly, like crushed stones, but there was an undercurrent of something else—curiosity or perhaps concern.

"Neither is life around here," she shot back, her tone sharper than she intended. What was she doing? Playing this game with a man who had seen the depths of darkness? He wouldn't be fooled by bravado. It wasn't the first time she had approached someone in desperate need of answers, and it certainly wouldn't be the last.

She remembered her first case—years ago, when she was just starting out as a PI. The thrill of the chase, the innocence of belief coupled with a naivety that had long since eroded. Back then, chasing down leads felt like playing detective in a world of black and white, where every shadow hinted at some hidden truth. But the city had taught her that truth was often veiled and sometimes, even deceptive.

The bartender glanced at her, and she could see the gears turning in his mind. The lines around his mouth deepened as he considered her, pouring another glass of amber liquid. "Got some questions about a missing girl, huh?"

Elena straightened, her heart racing; she had finally pulled on a thread. "Yeah. She's a socialite from uptown. A woman by the name of Ava Sinclair."

He leaned forward, resting his forearms atop the bar, eyes gleaming with cautious interest. "Ava? Sure, I've heard whispers. Lots of folks have, but 'round here, whispers don't mean much."

"Whispers can sometimes lead to the truth." Elena felt a sense of urgency creeping into her voice. She didn't want to scare him off, but every second mattered. The clock was ticking, and with every moment spent here, the case grew colder.

"Maybe," he replied, almost thoughtfully. "But you've gotta know how to listen. And here, the stories ain't always what they seem."

Elena leaned in closer, lowering her voice to match the conspiratorial atmosphere that hung in the room. "Tell me what you know."

The bartender took a long swig from his glass before setting it down with a determined thud. "Ava was seen last week, roaming around these parts. Quite the sight—a posh girl in a joint like this, you know?"

"Do you know who she was with?"

He shook his head slowly, a wry smile curling at the edges of his lips. "Not exactly a good crowd. Shows up here once in a blue moon, looking for something—or someone—she thinks she lost."

"What do you mean?"

"Rumors," he muttered, a hand waving dismissively as if brushing aside the very idea that he had even mentioned them. "She's got a wandering eye and a taste for trouble, but... trouble isn't the half of it."

The bartender paused, watching as Elena's expression shifted from curiosity to intent. The shadows of her past rose within her, intertwining with the heaviness in the air. For every customer he served, there was a story of pain and expectations dashed against the jagged rocks of reality.

"What does that mean?" she pressed, aware of the emotions she was dredging up.

"I've heard things," he drawled, leaning back against the bar, his hard demeanor softening momentarily. "Rumors of a bar backdoor deal—an artist and a socialite. Love, betrayal, or so the story goes. Ava was entangled in something deep."

Images of the tortured artist from her earlier investigation danced in Elena's mind—a man who poured his heart and soul onto canvas, perhaps in exchange for something far more lucrative than mere admiration. An emotional connection or something darker? Her heartbeat quickened as a thread began to unravel.

"An artist?" she echoed, the name playing on the edges of her thoughts. "You know him?"

The bartender hesitated, scanning the room for listeners. "There's a few names tossed around. But if you're looking for the truth, you might want to look at Simon Hale. Word is, he knows more than he lets on."

"Where can I find him?"

"He usually haunts the galleries uptown—when he's not lost in a bottle, that is." The bartender's eyes glimmered with mischief, a small smile creeping onto his lips.

With her notepad in hand, Elena scribbled the artist's name, her mind racing with possibilities. Would this be the connection she needed to crack the case wide open? Or would it lead her into a deeper abyss?

Every fragment of information fell into place, unearthing memories she had buried. The bar around her faded, and nostalgia washed over her like a tide.

This world, with its dirty secrets and reckless hearts, she knew all too well. The dark corners of life had always felt like home, where everyone was tangled up in lies that chained them to their past. She had found her footing among these shadows, where the truth had a peculiar way of hiding just beneath the surface, and every soul here had a battle to fight.

But there were haunted stories in her past. Once, she had trusted too easily, walking the line between life and the murky depths of deceit. Although she was no longer that green investigator who chased after every whisper, the dim bar mirrored the swirling aftermath of past events that crept beneath her skin.

The bartender's voice snapped her back to reality. "I can't help you get to Simon, but I can tell you that he's lost just as much as she is. They both had expectations, drowned in the same bottle."

"Expectations?" Elena echoed, focusing on his words, piecing together the fleeting images of their mutual past. If Ava and Simon shared a connection, then perhaps it gestated in some unrequited need that led them down dark paths.

"Can't expect a flame to stay lit forever when all you have is a flickering candle," he continued, studying her carefully. "You find yourself choking on smoke more often than you care to admit."

His eyes pierced through her, as if searching for her own scars. **Smoke.** It wafted like specters, reminding her of the missteps she had made—the ghosts of her lovers and partners clouding her vision with each emotional entanglement. She shivered, wishing she could drown the memories in whiskey. Yet she forced herself to nod, to engage with him further. "Can you tell me more about their past?"

"Listen, sweetheart. The streets are buzzing about them. Artists are sensitive creatures. They wear their hearts on their sleeves, and Simon's sleeves have bled heavily for Ava." He gave her a half-hearted smirk. "Always wanted to save her from herself, but you know how it goes. She dabbled with fire—too much, too close."

"Do you think she's in trouble?"

"Trouble finds everyone in this city, doesn't it?" His shrug was casual, but there was an edge of caution woven in his words. "Ava's just a piece in a much bigger puzzle."

Pieces began to click into place in Elena's mind, the faces of the city's elite mingling with those of the shadowed figures she encountered. Access and influence, along with betrayal—those were dangerous cocktails crafted by the desperate.

"Where do I find Simon?"

"Could be at the Starlight Gallery tonight." He paused, his eyes flicking back towards the room behind her. "But the thing about galleries… it brings a crowd. Careful who you approach. You might end up tangled in a web of his own creation."

A web. The strands of intrigue around her thickened and tightened, revealing an entanglement that spun deeper than she realized.

"Thanks," she said, already slipping a couple of bills onto the bar.

As she turned to leave, he called after her. "One more thing, Elena. Sometimes rumors are born from pain; sometimes they're just smoke. Gotta know which is which."

She nodded, absorbing every word before stepping back into the night. The cool air rushed over her, a stark contrast to the warmth of the crowded bar. Each stride away from the building reminded her of the fragility of trust, and the bittersweet allure of secrets that others kept.

She felt drawn to the upcoming gallery, not for its charm, but for the allure of unraveling a deeper connection in a twist of fate that bound her to a missing woman and an artist desperately brandishing his demons on the canvas.

As she navigated the neon-lit streets, faint whispers echoed in her mind, leading her onward.

They were the whispers of the night, the warnings mingled with hopes, the trepidation that came with longing. Trust was a cruel mistress—a sweet, dark thread that offered comfort only to gnaw at you when least expected.

She stepped into her past again, threaded with the complexities of love, tragedy, and regret, prepared to pay the price for the truth she sought. The city remained elusive, its secrets pulsing like the heartbeat of a living entity, but she was ready to unearth what lay hidden beneath its surface. Little did she know that the shadows bore witness to the tangled lines of loyalty, desire, and betrayal, each lingering with a dark promise of their own.

As she moved into the heart of the city, she embraced the one constant that had propelled her forward—the unquenchable quest for knowledge, for respect, and for an understanding of those who fell victim to the very shadows that had veiled them.

The First Clue

As the last hints of evening light slipped away, the smoky haze of the bar coiled around Elena Rourke like an embrace—both familiar and suffocating. The dimness beneath the flickering neon lights seemed to pulse with the heartbeat of the city, each shadow concealing a whisper, a laugh, or a sigh steeped in hidden narratives. She surveyed her surroundings, scrutinizing the ebb and flow of patrons consumed by their petty dramas and bottled truths.

The clinking of glasses and the low hum of conversation enveloped her, blending into a background symphony that felt both spirited and haunting. In the far corner, a group of men laughed too loudly, their bravado disguising a desperation that blended seamlessly with the bar's peeling paint and the air thick with old secrets.

She took a sip of her whiskey, letting the warmth seep through her, and focused on the murmurings of a place alive with hints—hints that formed the contours of her investigation.

Elena had made it her mission to find the missing socialite, a woman who had seemingly vanished into the shadows of the same city that birthed her charm and elegance. The missing woman's world—filled with glamour, privilege, and public adoration—had become a distant echo. As she observed the scenes unfolding around her, she felt a surge of determination surge within her; she was close—she could feel it.

It was then that her gaze was drawn to a soft glimmer nestled amid the gum-stained floorboards that echoed stories of greater importance. Curious, she pushed through the crowd that clustered around a pool table and followed the flickering light. As she knelt down to take a closer look, her heart raced; there it lay, shimmering defiantly against a backdrop of urban decay—a delicate silver bracelet.

The bracelet was adorned with tiny, intricate leaves, each one designed to catch the light, twisting just so to reflect a fleeting beauty—a stark contrast to its surroundings. But it was more than just a piece of jewelry; it was a relic, an artifact that carried the weight of the woman's life. The craftsmanship spoke volumes, revealing a desperate search for something untouchable, lost among the chaos of an unforgiving world.

Elena's fingers caressed the cool, polished metal as she picked it up, her breath catching in her throat. She had seen this bracelet before—there was no doubt. It had hung delicately on the wrist of Sarah Delacroix, the missing socialite, at countless high-profile charity galas and exclusive events.

This very piece had glimmered under the gaudy lights of the city's elite, draping elegance across wrists that held untold stories and hidden fears.

But how had it ended up here, discarded like a fallen star?

The discovery was bittersweet, igniting an ember of hope in her chest, yet casting a shadow of dread across her mind. It was a clue—a tangible piece to the puzzle that had eluded her. She had no time to waste. As she slipped the bracelet into her pocket, she scanned the room, her instincts sharpening, aware that this might draw the attention of those who thrived in the city's underbelly.

The bar was no longer just a den of inebriation and refuge; it had morphed into a tangled web of potential connections, informants, and threads of intrigue. She needed to dig deeper, to unearth the narrative locked behind these walls. With a newfound sense of purpose, she navigated toward the bar, each step calculated.

The bartender, a weathered man with deep-set eyes that observed everything and missed nothing, stood polishing a glass, seemingly oblivious to the world swirling around him. His name was Dave, a fixture in the neighborhood, and a reluctant keeper of secrets. Though he was loath to share, on occasions when the moon hung high and fortune favored the bold, he could be persuaded.

"Hey, Dave," Elena greeted, forcing a casual tone as she slid onto the barstool, "got a second?"

He glanced up from his chore, arching a brow. "Your usual wouldn't be sufficient?"

"Not tonight. I'm looking for something a bit more… interesting."

"Interesting, huh? What's that supposed to mean?" His lips curled into a knowing smirk, but he leaned back, a hint of curiosity glinting in his eyes.

Elena hesitated for half a heartbeat, weighing her options. Would mentioning the bracelet tip the balance, drawing unwanted attention? Or was this enough to pry open the cautious door of conversation?

"I think I've found something that could lead me to the truth about Sarah's disappearance," she finally admitted, biting back her nerves as excitement flickered in her chest.

Dave set the glass down, leaning closer. "That so? And what makes you think you'll find anything in this cesspool?"

"This cesspool," she chuckled softly, "might just be the key to moving from whispers to truths."

He studied her for a moment, then nodded slowly. "Alright then. What have you got?"

Elena took the bracelet out, placing it delicately on the bar between them. As Dave's eyes widened, she seized the moment.

"I found this… on the floor. Sarah wore it. Do you know anything about it? Where it might've come from? What it might mean?"

His gaze flicked from the bracelet to her, cautious, then back to the delicate piece of silver that shimmered under the dim light. "It's a nice piece, no doubt. But it's hard to say just how it ended up here."

She leaned in, her voice barely above a whisper, "I'm not asking for your secrets, Dave. But you've seen your fair share; you know the whispers that float in here. Someone has to have seen something."

The bartender sighed, pulling away from the bar slightly as if to assert his boundaries. "You know how it goes, Elena. This place is no library. People come and go, their stories lost amidst beer spills and scuffles. You catch someone's glimpse of trouble, and it's gone before you even lift a finger."

"But this is different," Elena pressed. "Someone must know something. If I can connect the bracelet to Sarah, it could lead me to her. I need a name, a place, a connection."

"I can't promise anything." Dave kept his eyes on the bracelet, a shadow crossing his features.

"Just anything. I can't do this alone."

There it was—her vulnerability laid bare, a cornered predator showing her wounds in hopes of sympathy. In this world, she was just another shadow primed to become a meal for the hungry.

"Fine," he agreed gruffly, leaning back as if anticipating her next move. "There's a guy—Oliver. He comes in here every now and then. Claims to be a photographer. Says he knew Sarah before the big lights got to her head."

"Oliver?" Elena repeated, the name swirling in her mind. She had heard whispers about him. An artist with a reputation for portraying beauty from chaos—a tortured spirit wrapped in layers of flair and pretension. "Where can I find him?"

"I see him around here often. Wouldn't call him reliable, though. Got a tendency to get lost in his own world—like he's always searching for something just out of reach."

Elena leaned closer, determination surging through her veins. "And what if I'm that something?"

"Then you're in for a ride, Elena. Just be careful. Curiosity and hunger for truth can lead a girl into dark alleys she might not come back from."

The caution laced in his voice struck a chord; a smirk danced on his lips, hinting at the dangers that dwelled in shadows and light. As she pondered the words, her gaze flickered back to the bracelet, its shimmering surface begging for answers.

"Where can I find this Oliver?" she asked, pressing forward before he could withdraw into his shell.

"He spends most days wandering the art district—creeping around those cafes that are more about the ambiance than actual coffee. If you're lucky, you might catch him daydreaming at Parcelle on Smith Street. But, like I said, he's an elusive one."

"Thanks, Dave," Elena replied, determination fueling her next steps. As she pushed herself off the stool, she felt the bracelet's weight in her pocket—a promise of clues waiting to unfurl, intertwined with the threads of her investigation and the connections she hoped to forge.

Slipping into the cool night air, the neon lights flickered with a vibrancy she hadn't noticed before. The city bustled with life, each corner echoing with laughter and secrets.

The pulse of her surroundings resonated with her growing anticipation, an electric current guiding her deeper into the unknown.

The alleyways unfolded with an air of urgency. As she threaded her way through the labyrinthine streets, the atmosphere shifted from the comforting haze of the bar to the breathless anticipation of discovery. With each stride, her thoughts danced with fragments of possibilities—the bracelet's history, the path it would take her down, and the eventual unveiling of the missing socialite's fate.

Reaching the art district, the aroma of fresh paint and artisan goods washed over her, mingling with flashes of creativity that hung in the air. The streets were district alive with color, splashes of vibrancy competing for attention amidst the gray concrete. Art was a language she understood, a medium through which emotions flowed, and tonight, she sought to translate the static into a narrative that made sense.

Parcelle greeted her like an old friend, with its wooden tables strewn over the sidewalk and candles flickering against the encroaching dusk. A gathering place for dreamers, creators, and whispered ambitions, it offered her a window into the world she was now desperate to understand.

As she stepped inside, a surge of creativity enveloped her. The walls adorned with local art vibrated with energy, each piece beckoning with stories waiting to be unveiled. Salient voices danced in harmony, punctuated by the clinking of cups and the rustle of art books. This was where she might find Oliver, and with him, perhaps the threads that would unravel her tightly-woven mystery.

Sure enough, as she navigated the eclectic mix of patrons, her gaze settled on a solitary figure tucked away in a corner booth, deep in conversation with a canvas of his own design. Oliver was a striking man, his tousled hair framing his angular jaw and piercing blue eyes. He seemed lost in the art before him, paint from discarded palettes coating his hands, a gentle reminder of his passion—a passion that had undoubtedly once flickered in the eyes of Sarah Delacroix,

It took little more than a glance for Elena to realize he was an artist wrestling with visages of beauty and pain, elements mingling on the edges of creation. With a deep breath, she stepped forward, ready to confront whatever ghosts lingered in his shadows.

"Oliver?" she called, weaving through the people cluttering the space. His gaze lifted, uncertainty knitting his brows.

"Depends on who's asking," he replied cautiously, almost defensively.

"Elena Rourke, private investigator. I need to talk to you about Sarah Delacroix."

The mention of the name cracked the façade of nonchalance around him, his expression sombering as he processed her words. "Sarah… She's missing, isn't she?" The weight of grief cast a pall over his features, exposing vulnerability beneath the surface of bravado.

"That's exactly why I'm here," she assured him, taking the seat across from him. "I found something that belonged to her."

Pulling the bracelet from her pocket, she placed it on the table between them, the silvery structure gleaming in the soft light—a beacon worthy of attention amid a sea of mundane conversations.

Oliver's breath caught, and he shifted forward, eyes narrowing as recognition washed over him. "I know that piece. It was a gift from her mother—one of her favorites."

"What can you tell me about her? About your relationship?"

The artist's demeanor shifted; tension rippled through him as he regarded the bracelet like a ghost from a past life. "We dated for a while," he admitted, his voice laden with nostalgia. "But things got complicated as she climbed the social ladder. I wasn't part of that world."

"What do you mean?"

"Sarah had dreams, and she was good at achieving them. But sometimes the pursuit of dreams makes you lose sight of the things that matter—the people in your life." Each word was measured, as if pulling them from a wellspring of introspection. "When the glamour took over, I became a shadow in her story."

Elena could feel the weight of regret, the tethering threads of emotion binding him to a past he could not escape. "Did you ever think she might end up in trouble?"

He raked fingers through his hair, the movement a show of frustration. "I wish I could say yes, but the truth is, I lost touch long before her disappearance. I only heard whispers."

"Whispers?" she pressed.

"People in her circle are fiercely protective, and when she went missing, the murmurs of jealousy, betrayal, and fear spread like wildfire. They all wanted to take part in her glamor but never glanced back to see who they stepped on."

Elena regarded him, piecing together fragments of his words. "Do you have any names? Anyone who was close to her before her disappearance?"

He hesitated, lost in thought, then replied, "There was a party—one of her last. She began distancing herself from old friends, but I heard she had a showdown with a woman named Lorelei—a fellow socialite. They had a history."

"Lorelei? What do you know about her?"

"Rich, spoiled, with connections deep in the underbelly of the elite. Never satisfied, always in the light, one of the main players in the high society drama." The bitterness laced his words, a reflection of Elana's own sentiments toward the shimmering facade of wealth and privilege. "I don't think she ever liked Sarah. There was envy in Lorelei's eyes every time they crossed paths."

"Anything else?"

"Just rumors. Lorelei dealt with dangerous company, men who knew how to play the game. You might want to tread carefully."

"Thank you, Oliver," she said softly, noting the gravity of his warnings. As their conversation drew to a close, she felt the puzzle pieces slowly falling into place.

"Stay safe, Elena," he uttered, watching her rise from the table, every unguarded expression reflecting his concern. "The city has a way of absorbing those who tread too deeply."

"Trust me, this isn't the end of the line," she assured, tucking the bracelet back into her pocket as she departed, embracing the weight of their exchange, the pulse of the city drawing her deeper into its tangled embrace.

The night felt charged with potential as she stepped back into the sprawling streets buzzing with life and chaos. Everything was both familiar and terrifyingly new. Each den of secrets she passed seemed to hum with allure and danger, a reminder that she was navigating a labyrinth woven with human desires and shadows.

With the jewelry clinking softly in her pocket and the thread of connection entwining her with Oliver and Lorelei, her path was set, and determination coursed through her veins. The answers were lurking just beyond reach, tangled in shadows, waiting for her to uncoil them.

As she walked toward her next lead, the city—a tumultuous blend of hope and despair—revealed itself as both a labyrinth and a sanctuary, pulling her further into its enigmatic depths. The journey had only just begun.

The Allure of Sin

Meeting the Femme Fatale

The warm glow of golden chandeliers overhead bathed the opulent hotel lounge in a soft, inviting light. Elena Rourke stepped through the arching doorway, the luxurious scents of aged whiskey and jasmine mingling in the air. She surveyed the scene around her, taking in the polished wood bar and the plush, velvet couches that lined the walls like sentinels watching over whispered conversations. It was a world of elegance and excess, a sanctuary for the affluent and the mysterious. Every detail screamed indulgence: the rich fabrics, the delicate crystal glassware, and the low hum of a jazz trio setting a sultry mood throughout the room.

Yet, beneath the polished surface of this luxury, an underlying tension pulsed through the space, a tension that matched the unsettled whirlwind in Elena's heart. She was here on business—an investigation into a missing socialite who had been seen last mingling among the very elite that filled this lounge—but she could feel the magnetic allure of the place drawing her in, tugging at her resolve.

As her eyes adjusted to the dim light, they landed on a woman seated at the far end of the bar. Clad in a sleek, emerald-green dress that clung to her form like a second skin, the woman possessed an otherworldly beauty that seemed to absorb the very light around her. Her dark hair fell in cascading waves over one shoulder, framing a face that was strikingly symmetrical yet entirely captivating.

The light caught the high points of her cheekbones, illuminating the smooth, flawless complexion. But it was her eyes—an intense and piercing green—that truly ensnared Elena's fascination. They sparkled with a cunning intelligence, promising secrets yet to be revealed.

Elena took a deep breath, steeling herself against the unexpected flutter in her chest, and approached the bar. The woman turned slightly at the sound of Elena's footsteps, and their eyes locked for a moment. It was a brief connection, charged with a flicker of recognition that sent an electric current through Elena.

"Can I buy you a drink?" Elena asked, her voice steady despite the excitement bubbling beneath the surface.

The woman smiled, a slow, sultry curl of her lips that seemed to keep a hundred confidences hidden. "I would be disappointed if you didn't." Her voice was smooth, velvety, wrapped in an accent that suggested sophistication and worldly experience. "But I must warn you, I'm not the kind of company one usually seeks out for casual conversation."

Elena felt a rush of anticipation mingled with unease. "I'm not easily frightened."

"Oh, darling," the woman replied, her gaze sliding over Elena with a measured intensity before returning to meet her eyes. "I never suggested fear as a deterrent."

Elena smirked, intrigued. Everyone in this city played with masks, and she had learned to navigate the complexities of their facades.

Yet something about this femme fatale felt different—her charm was intoxicating, with hints of danger simmering just below the surface.

As they settled into plush chairs near the bar, Elena noted the understated elegance of the woman's movements. There was an effortless grace to the way she gestured, her long fingers drawing attention to the delicate rings adorning them, glinting in the warm light. "I'm Elena," she introduced herself, conscious of how she leaned forward slightly, drawn in by this enigma.

"Vivienne," the woman responded, her smile broadening. "A pleasure to meet you, Elena."

Elena could feel the intoxicating aura surrounding Vivienne as they began to converse. A slight flick of her wrist sent the bartender into action, and a moment later, two crystal glasses filled with deep crimson liquid appeared before them. "A specialty tonight," Vivienne purred, raising her glass in a subtle toast. "To serendipitous encounters."

"To serendipitous encounters," Elena echoed, taking a sip. The liquid burned smoothly down her throat, igniting a warmth that coursed through her, awakening her senses.

"The missing socialite," Vivienne remarked casually, as if reading Elena's thoughts. The air shifted, and Elena felt as though a spotlight had been turned on her. "You're investigating her disappearance, aren't you?"

"No one misses much in a place like this," Elena replied, keeping her tone light, even as her heartbeat quickened. "You seem quite well-informed."

"It's a small world, dear. The wealthy have their ways of communicating." Vivienne leaned back in her chair, her eyes glinting with mischief. "People in high places often forget that their shadows stretch long. One can always find the semblance of truth beneath layers of opulence."

Elena cocked her head, intrigued by the breadth of Vivienne's knowledge. "And what do you know of the socialite?"

The smile faded slightly from Vivienne's lips, replaced by a contemplative look that hinted at buried memories. "Margaux LaRue was a friend of mine—an extraordinary woman, full of life and light. Unfortunately, she also danced with danger, basking too long in a spotlight that could prove blinding."

The subtle shift in Vivienne's demeanor was not lost on Elena. It felt as though they were unraveling more than mere words; they were stripping away layers of pretense, exposing the raw emotions lingering beneath.

"She had her battles, as we all do," Vivienne continued, her voice barely above a whisper. "But her greatest struggle was with trust. It's an ephemeral thing in our circles… easily given, yet so easily shattered."

Elena observed the woman closely, sensing that Vivienne possessed more wisdom than mere gossip alone could yield. "And what would you suggest I explore, if trust is so fragile?"

A flicker of amusement played across Vivienne's lips. "Seek the truth in whispers, where loyalty dances a fine line with betrayal. Look to the people she surrounded herself with—the lovers, the friends.

They bear the weight of her shadows. And you must decide who in that mix is worth trusting."

Elena leaned forward, caught between her professional curiosity and an undeniable attraction igniting within her. "You speak openly of danger, yet I find you dangerously compelling."

"Isn't that the art of seduction?" Vivienne replied, her tone laced with playful sincerity. The tension between them thickened, vibrating with an unspoken promise that both excited and challenged Elena.

"And who is to say that you are not the true danger?"

"Oh, Elena," Vivienne said, extending her hand across the table, fingers lightly brushing against Elena's. "You'll have to discern that for yourself. Sometimes, in order to find the truth, one must be willing to tread dangerously close to the flames."

With each word, Elena felt the safety she once clung to begin to erode. Vivienne's charm was intoxicating, a seductive trap wrapped in silk and satin, offering nothing but the promise of unknown depths to explore. Yet there, too, lay the looming threat—a paradox that made this encounter as thrilling as it was precarious.

"I'm not afraid of a little fire," Elena stated, her voice steady, emboldened by the challenge.

Vivienne leaned back, a smirk painting her lips. "Perhaps that's what makes you so enthralling."

The air between them crackled with unresolved tension, igniting an electric undercurrent that could lead to either danger or revelation.

As they navigated their lively exchange, the world around them faded, and nothing existed but the two of them and the veils of intrigue that hung thick in the air.

Suddenly, the moment fractured like glass, when a group of raucous laughter erupted from a nearby table. Elena's eyes instinctively darted away, breaking the magnetic hold that had ensnared her attention on Vivienne.

"Ah, the rabble," Vivienne remarked, her tone dripping with elegance. "Always seeking to intrude on fine moments."

Still in a stupor from their charged conversation, Elena shifted back to Vivienne, who now wore an unreadable expression. "Do you fear them?" Elena asked.

"Fear?" Vivienne's laughter rang like a chiming bell, harboring mystery and mischief. "No, darling. Fear is for those unwilling to confront their demons. I prefer to embrace the chaos that comes with knowing who I truly am."

And therein lay the crux of it—the temptation in Vivienne's presence felt like drawing nearer to an abyss where truth intertwined with shadows. Elena's instincts screamed at her to flee, but her morbid curiosity made her linger on the precipice, teetering between caution and the allure of the unknown.

"Perhaps I'm feeling adventurous tonight," Elena replied, leaning back in her chair, her heartbeat drumming with anticipation.

"Ah, adventurism. A dangerous game, especially when lives hang in the balance."

"Yet here we are, playing it," Elena said, her voice a soft challenge.

"Indeed." Vivienne raised her glass, her eyes glinting with mischief. "To reckless pursuits, then."

"To reckless pursuits," Elena echoed, their glasses clinking in a resounding toast. The taste of the drink on her lips felt like a promise, one that invigorated her very senses and heightened her awareness.

Vivienne's gaze intensified, and she leaned closer, the distance between them narrowing as she lowered her voice into an inviting whisper. "But remember, dear Elena, every choice comes with a price. You have the chance to leave this moment behind. The question is, will you?"

Elena met her probing stare, her heart racing at the realization that they were no longer merely two women meeting by chance. They were explorers in a treacherous territory of unguarded emotions—hunters and prey caught in a delicate dance where every step could tip the scales toward danger.

"Perhaps I crave the adrenaline of the chase," Elena mused, matching Vivienne's intensity, testing the waters of this uncertain intimacy.

With a low chuckle, Vivienne's demeanor transformed into something both playful and dangerously alluring. "You misunderstand, my dear. It is not just a chase I offer, but an expedition into the heart of shadows. Are you ready to face what lurks within?"

Elena felt the shivers of uncertainty dance down her spine, her ambitions clashing with the undeniable pull of attraction that rippled within her.

"Show me, then," she replied, her spirit alight with daring. The initial interaction had become a seductive game, and with each twist, Elena could sense the stakes growing higher.

"Very well," Vivienne said, her voice dropping to a sultry murmur that dripped temptation. "But know that once the door to darkness is opened, returning is rarely as simple. Just remember that not all shadows are unkind."

As Elena sat captivated by Vivienne's magnetic presence, she realized she was on the precipice of entering a world painted in shades of sin and seduction—a step that could lead her closer to the truth behind the socialite's disappearance, or deeper into a labyrinth of deceit.

The ambiance around them simmered with newfound energy, enriched by the unspoken understanding that their paths were irreversibly intertwined in a dance of trust, desire, and treachery. Elena understood that the captivating femme fatale before her was not only an ally to seek but also a potential adversary in an unforgiving game where every glance and subtle smile could mask the chilling truths of burgeoning desire.

As they exchanged smiles—a fusion of challenge and invitation—the air thickened with an unnameable promise, driving them both further into the magnetic pull that would soon redefine the rules of their own game.

And with that, Elena realized that navigating this seductive maze was not merely about discovering the truth; it was about confronting her own shadows and the desire that lingered just beneath the surface.

When the lights dimmed slightly, casting silhouettes against the richly adorned walls of the lounge, Elena felt as if she stood between two worlds—one of certainty and order, and the other, wild and untamed, beckoning her toward its depths. The choice lay before her, and at that moment, she knew she was ready to embrace its allure, even if it meant stepping into the embrace of shadows,
spilling secrets that could change everything.

Seduction in the Shadows

Elena sank deeper into the plush embrace of the hotel lounge, the golden hues of the chandeliers reflecting off the glasses of champagne that glimmered in front of her. The air was thick with the scent of indulgence, a intoxicating mix of expensive perfumes and the faintest hint of smoke from the occasional cigarette. Conversations wove around her like fine silk, muffled laughter dancing on the edges of hushed tones, creating a tapestry of sound that was at once alluring and disorienting.

Across the table, the femme fatale sat gracefully, her elegance almost ethereal under the rich light. Dressed in deep red, her outfit clung to her curves like a lover's embrace, exuding a magnetic charm that kept every gaze in the room locked towards her. She played with her drink, tracing the rim of the glass with an elongated finger, every movement deliberate and filled with an unspoken promise.

"You know, Elena," she said, her voice silky smooth, almost as if it could wrap around Elena like a velvet ribbon, "the truth is a terrible thing to waste. Especially in a place like this."

Elena's heart raced—a strange mix of excitement and apprehension coursing through her veins. This was not merely an investigation anymore; it was a heady game of cat and mouse in which both players were painfully aware of the thin line they tread between danger and desire.

"And what is it you think the truth might be?" Elena asked, trying to keep her tone steady, fighting the vulnerability she felt as she met the femme fatale's piercing gaze. The intensity of those eyes could devour the most stoic of souls, and yet, a part of Elena found herself craving to reveal the secrets that churned beneath the surface of her own heart.

The femme fatale leaned closer, her presence enveloping Elena, drawing her into a world that promised both tantalizing delights and perilous traps. "Truth can be like champagne, darling. Bubbly and exhilarating at first sip, but too much can leave you with a terrible hangover. Don't you find?"

Elena's laughter was weak, caught off guard by the brilliance of the metaphor. The femme fatale was offering insight wrapped in seductive mystery, and it was intoxicating.

"But isn't the hangover worth the thrill of the chase?" The question hung suspended between them, crackling with anticipation. Suddenly, the stakes of the investigation felt more personal, the fine line between fascination and danger began to blur further.

The soft thumping of music pulsed in the background, setting a rhythm that mirrored the shipwreck of desire that was slowly consuming Elena.

As the femme fatale continued to display the stories that were more alluring and dangerous with every sip of her drink, Elena felt her resolve softening, battered by the charm and energy radiating from the woman across the table.

"You want to know about Claudia, don't you? The missing socialite?" the femme fatale's voice dipped conspiratorially, her eyes sparkling with mischief.

The mention of Claudia sent a shiver into Elena's spine, awakening her instincts. This was why she had come—to uncover the truth that lay intricately entwined within the web of this femme fatale's world.

"I don't want a fairy tale, just the facts, the truth, no shadows between us," Elena replied, steeling her gaze, but still her breath caught in her throat as the femme fatale smirked.

"Oh, darling, facts are for journalists. We're here to explore the tantalizing—what if the truth is the greatest lie of all?" The femme fatale took a deep sip of her champagne, the bubbles dancing mockingly within the glass.

The tension between them stretched, each woman testing the other's resolve. All around, the world seemed to fade away—the soft clatter of dishes, the laughter, the music—until it felt like they existed in a pocket of time where desire sparked like fireworks amidst the shadows.

"Tell me a story then," Elena demanded, her curiosity deepening, her professional facade slowly peeling away. She leaned in slightly, her instincts buzzing, yearning to take the plunge into the depths of this alluring enigma.

And so, the femme fatale began.

"Once upon a time, in a city much like ours, a young woman fell into the arms of depravity. She was beautiful, intelligent—a creature of lust and passion, living on the edge of society's expectations. She had friends, lovers, and ties that she thought would protect her. But with power comes greed, and greed demands sacrifices, doesn't it?" Her voice dripped with seduction, each word carefully laced with spices of melancholy.

Elena felt herself corporeally transported into that world with the femme fatale as she wove her narrative. Each captivating phrase pulled her deeper into the implications of desire and betrayal that echoed so closely to her investigation. The atmosphere shifted, shadowy partners twirling in her mind, as the femme fatale continued.

"Claudia was that woman, you know. She danced with demons, was engaged with people of power. Her disappearance? Well, it's hardly surprising given the nature of her alliances. She played a dangerous game—a game I once played myself, where the stakes are measured in hearts broken and blood spilled. The price of beauty is steep, my dear."

Her words painted a vibrant canvas in Elena's mind, evoking images of Claudia smiling in elegance while surrounded by dark figures in the background, their faces shrouded in shadows. The imagery demanded to be deciphered, hinting at alliances both toxic and intoxicating.

"What do you imply?" Elena whispered, her voice almost a breath, captivated yet wary of where the femme fatale's tale might lead.

"Imply? Oh, sweet darling. In this world, implication is often stronger than fact. It's a dance of shadows—each step choreographed by those who wish to keep the truth hidden. But I imagine the pieces you chase, like Claudia, bear weight more than just their charm. They carry secrets meant to be buried." The femme fatale's gaze pierced Elena, breathing life into a fragile silence that echoed between them.

Elena fought to maintain her composure, aware of the layers of temptation wrapped up in the femme fatale's words. Conversations moved like smoke—ephemeral, curling into the air and leaving behind nothing but a subtle stain of the past—and Elena could feel herself drifting through that haze.

"Then tell me, what secrets does Claudia keep?" Elena queried, the hunter instinct glowing fiercely. She stoked the fire within her, igniting the desire to unearth, to understand despite the price attached to the truths she sought.

The femme fatale smiled knowingly, the playful curve of her lips igniting something dangerous in the air. "Perhaps secrets are best revealed not by direct inquiry but through the mischief of desire. What is it that you desire most, Elena? Success? Truth? Or something more… visceral?"

The targeted question landed heavily in the air, challenging the very foundation of Elena's ambitions. Her cheeks flushed under the intensity of the scrutiny—the battle within stoking the flame of her pursuit, a heady mixture of professional endeavor layered with forbidden desire.

But Elena was not so easily swayed. She wouldn't let her personal emotions sway the trajectory of her path. "I desire justice for Claudia. Nothing more. She deserves the truth, as do I."

In response, the femme fatale tilted her head slightly, those abyssal eyes holding a deeper understanding. "Justice, my dear, depends greatly on whose story you choose to believe. And believe me, there are many."

Intrigued, Elena leaned further into the conversation, an invisible tether pulling her forward, resistant yet vulnerable to the femme fatale's honeyed words. Every string of conversation sparked something lush within the recesses of Elena's heart, questioning the very foundation of her convictions.

"How do you know her? What's your relationship with her?" Elena pressed, trying to decipher the layers that remained hidden behind the femme fatale's mask of allure.

"Ah, my relationship? It weaves in and out like the moonlight—sometimes hidden, other times illuminated," she replied dreamily, tracing a finger along the rim of her glass. "Claudia was a friend, a confidante, and perhaps a bit more at times… But friendships in this intricate tapestry are rarely straightforward."

Elena's breath caught, the implications stirring a curiosity that threatened to unravel her focus. Was there more to Claudia's disappearance—the entanglement of emotions and desires that transcended the professional front Elena projected?

The femme fatale closed the distance further, her voice barely above a whisper.

"But friendships, just like truths, can morph and deceive. In my world, deception is but another shade of love, another thread in the grand design. Are you ready to play, Elena?"

Elena shivered slightly, her heart racing at the invitation wrapped in shadows. The proposition was as exhilarating as it was terrifying, leaving traces of anticipation hanging heavy in the air.

With a feigned confidence that almost felt real, Elena replied, "I'm always ready to uncover the truth—whatever it takes."

The femme fatale leaned back, a conspiratorial smile lingering on her lips. "Then let us toast to that, shall we?"

Glasses clinked softly, the sound reverberating like a promise amidst their burgeoning connection—a reminder of the delicate dance between ambition and allure. This game they were playing straddled a fine edge, where every word exchanged was both invitation and threat, simultaneously drawing them closer while surrounding them with danger.

As the conversations unfolded, the night wore on, taking them deeper into the labyrinth of each other's imperfections. Each story carried an intimacy that pushed against the boundaries of trust, and there was a strange comfort in it.

Elena found herself ensnared in the webs spun by the femme fatale—every whispered secret, every suggestive glance, hypnotizing in nature, making the stakes feel ever more perilous. What began as a simple investigation had morphed into a dance with desire, with every fabric of their interaction laced with intrigue and something more sacrilegious.

She longed to decipher the truths hidden behind the femme fatale's elegant facade, yet each revelation wrapped around her heart, binding her to the woman who embodied both seduction and danger. The tug-of-war between her instincts and intrigue intensified, every interaction an intoxicating game of passion and peril.

With every sip of champagne, they plummeted deeper into shadowy confessions. Lost in a realm where words held weight far beyond their meanings, Elena found herself questioning her motives, drawn irresistibly to the femme fatale who, like a siren, lured her into treacherous waters under the guise of companionship.

And the deeper they delved, the more Elena's desire grew—to know not just Claudia's truth but the heart of the femme fatale herself. In that moment, surrounded by opulence, she realized that the investigation was colliding dangerously with her own thirst for connection, truth, and the exquisite tension of a world where allure danced treacherously close to betrayal.

As the ballroom began to dim, shadows playing tricks with the flickering lights above, Elena felt as if she were standing at the precipice, yearning for answers while seduced by the intricacies of desire. Whatever path the investigation led her down, she knew that the allure of sin would forever linger in this dance of shadows, both binding and betraying in equal measure.

Unraveling Threads

The music in the hotel bar was soft, a sultry jazz tune that wove in and out of the muted conversations swirling around the dimly lit space. Shadows danced along the polished wooden bar top, reflecting the light from the ornate chandeliers above, their crystals refracting into a kaleidoscope of color.

For Elena Rourke, the atmosphere was intoxicating yet unnerving—the perfect backdrop for secrets to unfurl.

She perched on a high stool, her gaze anchored to the femme fatale seated across from her. This enigmatic woman was a portrait of allure and danger, adorned in a shimmering gown that caught the light like a siren luring sailors to a treacherous shore. The rich, deep hues of her attire mirrored the depths of her concealed past—a past that Elena was determined to plumb, even as warnings echoed in her mind.

"You're quite the investigator, aren't you, Elena?" the femme fatale said, a coy smile playing on her lips. Her dark hair framed her face like a halo of shadows, enhancing the allure of her piercing gaze, which seemed to see straight through Elena's carefully constructed barriers.

"I try to be," Elena replied, her voice steady despite the fluttering unease in her stomach. She had been drawn to this woman from the moment they had met, as if an invisible thread had pulled her closer. But the closer she got, the more she felt the pull of danger, tempting her to take that next step into uncharted territory.

With a sweeping gesture, the femme fatale signaled for another round of drinks, and the bartender, a rugged man with a knowing smile, placed two fluted glasses of champagne on the bar. The bubbles glinted like stars trapped in liquid, and as Elena raised her glass, she couldn't shake the feeling that she was drinking in deception, each sip embedding her deeper into a murky world she barely understood.

"Tell me about Seraphina," Elena suggested, her tone casual but her intent deliberate.

She had spent enough time uncovering layers of socialite lives to recognize the complexities that lay beneath the surface. The missing socialite was more than just a headline; she was a puzzle piece in a much larger picture.

The femme fatale's expression shifted, her smile faltering as a shadow crossed her features. "Seraphina was... free-spirited, captivating. People were drawn to her light, like moths to a flame. But there was darkness, too. Beneath that glittering exterior lay insecurities, fears that lurked in the corners of her mind."

Elena leaned in, senses heightened. It was the contrast—the light and dark—that intrigued her. "What kinds of fears?"

"The world can be so harsh, especially for someone like her."

A pause followed, heavy with unspoken words, and Elena felt a surge of determination to peel back the layers of this mysterious woman. "But you knew her. You were close to her," she encouraged, her voice smooth and coaxing.

The femme fatale's fingers toyed absently with the stem of her glass, the soft clinking punctuating the silence that stretched between them. "We were friends... of a sort. Our lives intertwined at the edges of society's fabric, but we were different threads entirely. She had everything—or so it seemed. I had nothing but dreams painted in shades of despair."

Another layer revealed, and Elena took careful note. "So you felt you had little in common?"

The woman sighed, a wistfulness creeping into her voice. "Not in the ways that matter.

We shared a darkness, but my demons weren't the same as hers. She sought validation in the arms of others; I drowned in my own sorrows. But we were both searching, I suppose."

Elena absorbed this, contemplating the fragile bond that had tied them together. Perhaps it was their shared quest for something beyond what society upheld—they were both women caught in a web of expectations, struggling to escape the confines of the lives they led.

"Do you think... She might have disappeared willingly?" Elena ventured cautiously. The question hung heavily in the air, as the femme fatale's eyes widened, a flicker of surprise challenging her practiced composure.

"To escape?" she echoed, the notion clearly taking her aback. Her lips tightened, as if weighing the very idea against the truth she lived within. "No, Seraphina was not one to shun her life. She loved the spotlight."

As the response tumbled out, Elena felt the ebb and flow of a deeper tumult beneath the calm surface, like a current running through still waters. She sensed the femme fatale was holding back, and Elena's instincts urged her to dig deeper.

"But what if the spotlight was too bright? What if the pressure of being perfect became unbearable?" Elena prodded gently, her soft tone urging the woman to relinquish her guard. The room felt colder, the laughter dimming around them, reducing the chatter to a ghostly whisper as tension twisted on the edges of their conversation.

The femme fatale's composure wavered, a slight tremor betraying her.

"I don't know what went through her mind in those final days. But I sensed something changing. She grew distant, as if she was standing on the edge of a precipice, testing the wind beneath her feet."

Elena found herself captivated, straddling the line between professional curiosity and an influx of something more personal. Was she merely a detective uncovering mysteries, or was she drawn to this woman's vulnerability in ways she had not yet acknowledged? The intimacy of their exchange invigorated her investigative instincts while embroiling her in an emotional entanglement that confused her purpose.

"You mentioned she was afraid. What was she afraid of?"

"Losing it all, perhaps. The very essence of herself—to change, and yet to stay the same. She feared the truth lurking beneath her image," the femme fatale replied, her voice low and trembling. "She was more than a pretty face, you know. Beneath all that glamour, there was a soul struggling for meaning."

As the words fell from her lips, Elena saw something flicker in the femme fatale's expression—a connection, a yearning. This was not merely about Seraphina; there was something deeper that extended to their own entangled lives.

Elena shifted slightly, leaning that much closer, gauging the emotional currents swirling between them. "You said you knew her intimately. Was there something specific that frightened her? Something that pushed her closer to the edge?"

The femme fatale hesitated, her gaze locking onto the swirling drink before her. "There were whispers, rumors.

The kind that follow someone like her, breeding wicked intentions. The city's elite can be cruel, and they will go to great lengths to conceal their secrets."

Elena felt a spark ignite within her—a launching point for all the unanswered questions that had sat heavily on her heart. "What kinds of rumors?"

The femme fatale's lips curled into a knowing smile, one that felt both inviting and foreboding. "Powerful men, their dark desires, all intertwined with a woman who found herself caught up in their world."

Elena leaned in, intrigued. "You mean... she was involved with someone powerful?"

"More than one, I'd imagine. Men who loved her—for a time. Their affections were fickle, though; they never stayed for long. She was... a thrilling escape, a flicker of light in their shadowy lives. But the thrill wanes, doesn't it? Darkness creeps back in, and it seems she became more of a liability than desired."

Elena's pulse quickened as she processed the implications. A string of powerful men, each with their own motives, secrets potent enough to tie a woman's fate to their whims. Each revelation tugged on her desire to peel back the layers, to grasp the truth buried in a world laden with deceit.

"Did you ever meet any of these men?" she asked, careful to maintain a neutral expression. She could feel the tension thickening in the air, like a charge ready to electrify their conversation.

The femme fatale laughed quietly, though it held little mirth. "Men like that don't usually make their presence known to someone like me. But once, I found myself at a gala, where Seraphina shone the brightest. It was exhilarating, to be part of such a world, but it was suffocating, too. The rules of engagement were suffused with danger."

"Danger?" Elena echoed, leaning forward.

"Women like us are puppets in their games, dear." The femme fatale leaned closer, her breath barely a whisper against Elena's ear. "When the music fades and the lights go out, the puppet show crumbles, and we're left with our tangled threads."

The intimacy of their exchange reached a fever pitch, a palpable electricity crackling between them. Elena felt the thrill of their shared vulnerability, laced with trepidation and the allure of darker truths. This was no longer just an investigation; it had transformed into a delicate dance of seduction and danger.

"What if they hold the key to her disappearance?" Elena posited, her tone low and conspiratorial.

The femme fatale shifted her gaze, scrutinizing Elena for something—trust, perhaps. "Men like that have their eyes on bigger prizes, love. They rarely deal in whispers. But Seraphina was always in the crosshairs of their games."

With each word, Elena could feel the complexity of their relationship, woven together by shared secrets and unspoken fears. They were both dancers on a tightrope, teetering between trust and betrayal, and the allure of unearthing their own hidden truths.

"What if the truth is too dangerous to uncover?" Elena asked, letting the tension stretch between them like a coiled spring.

The femme fatale's lips curved into a provocative smile, daring Elena to wade further into the waters of uncertainty. "Then we dance, my dear. In the shadows where trust becomes a fleeting illusion. Our greatest strength is also our greatest weakness."

The hotel bar pulsed around them—a sanctuary filled with smoke, laughter, and secrets shadowed by the allure of desire. In the midst of it, Elena found herself inexplicably drawn to the femme fatale, entangled in a web of intimacy and intrigue.

As the night wore on, each question birthed ten more. The femme fatale had become an inadvertent guide through the labyrinthine corridors of Seraphina's life—a life punctuated by highs and lows, illuminated by moments of beauty but overshadowed by whispers of deceit. The intoxication within her glass mirrored her burgeoning fascination, blurring the lines between duty and desire.

Days turned to nights, and nights blended into an eternal twilight for Elena, who dug deeper into the seduction of shadows filling her mind. Yet within the allure lay a throbbing uncertainty, a tension that was both exciting and perilous. Every detail she uncovered brought her closer to truths buried beneath secrets, pushing her into a world she could barely navigate.

In her heart, she knew the dangers that loomed on the horizon, yet a part of her craved to be tumbling into the unknown. And the femme fatale—a being stitched together by mystery and allure—was the catalyst that ignited her yearning to untangle the life of a lost socialite, even as it threatened her very own.

The allure of ambition entwined with the danger of intimacy shaped her pursuit. Each thread pulled her deeper into an abyss brimming with shadows, drawing the contours of desire and deception ever closer together. Elena Rourke would forge ahead into that abyss, unraveling the mysteries entwined in the femme fatale's eyes, even as the dance of shadows became a reflection of her own intimate journey through the treachery of trust.

A Society of Lies

The Glistening Facade

The gala stretched before her like an opulent painting, the canvas filled with dreams and desires glittering under the grand chandeliers that flickered overhead. Each light cast a warm glow over the expansive ballroom, but beneath the illumination lay a darker truth, one that Elena Rourke was determined to uncover. Clad in an exquisite emerald gown that hugged her curves perfectly, she stepped through the ornate entrance with a confidence that masked her unease. The whispers of the elite filled the air, a symphony of laughter and clinking glasses that created a false sense of camaraderie.

As she navigated through the neatly arranged clusters of guests, Elena allowed her eyes to wander, absorbing the excesses of wealth displayed in the extravagance of the gala's decor. Silk drapes cascaded from the ceiling, drowning the walls in a sea of rich hues, while gilded mirrors reflected the myriad of jewels that adorned the attendees.

It was a scene designed to dazzle, a fleeting mirage that obscured the grim realities lurking beneath the shimmering surface.

Her mind flickered back to the case that had led her here—to find a missing socialite, a woman whose life had once shone brightly among this elite circle. There was an unshakeable connection between the vibrant visual feast surrounding her and the darkness she sought to unravel. What secrets were hidden beneath all this glamour?

Elena maneuvered gracefully, a smile gracefully painted over her lips, though her heart raced with each step deeper into the fray. Suddenly, her gaze caught on a group of women huddled together, their laughter high and thin like crystal bells. They draped in gowns that sparkled like freshly fallen stars, yet their eyes darted around, assessing the rivals that surrounded them. She noted their passive-aggressive glances, their whispers laced with brittle charm, a clear exhibition of the societal games played at such gatherings.

"Elena!" a voice called, slicing through the cacophony. It belonged to Vivienne Caldwell, a noted philanthropist and one of the most influential women in the city. She wore a gown of deep cobalt-blue that accentuated her striking features and fine jewelry that had surely been borrowed from a bank vault.

"Vivienne," Elena replied, sliding into the warm embrace of familiarity. Vivienne's presence was overwhelming yet welcoming, a goddess amidst mere mortals, and Elena felt a surge of urgency; this encounter could yield information.

"I didn't expect to see you here, darling. Are you investigating again?" Vivienne's tone dipped to a conspiratorial whisper, her eyes glinting with intrigue and amusement. "I must say, it suits you."

Elena maintained her smile but noted the flicker of calculation behind Vivienne's charm. "I've heard the party of the season tends to bring out the most… colorful characters."

"Colorful indeed!" Vivienne laughed lightly, though the sound carried an edge of something harsher. "But tread carefully, regardless of how intoxicating it may appear. Beneath the glitter and glamour lies a treachery you might not see coming."

A shiver raced down Elena's spine, igniting her instincts further. Here was a key in the vast lock of deceit she sought to unravel. But was Vivienne warning her out of genuine concern or merely asserting her dominance in the social hierarchy? Elena's instincts told her to play the game.

"What warnings do you have?" Elena asked, deliberately maintaining the intriguing tone.

Vivienne leaned closer, her voice dropping once more. "They know you're here, you realize? Some would rather keep their secrets buried than let a determined investigator meddle. Pay attention to who your allies are, dear. Beneath the glitz, there lurks danger."

Elena forced an easy laugh, suppressing the rising apprehension in her gut. "What's life without a little danger, Vivienne?"

"True words," Vivienne agreed, her eyes narrowing thoughtfully. "Just remember—everyone here wears their armor to conceal the cracks in their facade. Most have more to lose than their smiles alone."

As Vivienne floated away into the throng of glittering socialites, Elena felt the weight of her warning resonate in her mind. She carefully scanned the room, assessing the attendees who wore their façade as skillfully as their designer outfits. Beneath the laughter, she sensed an air of tension, a low hum of competition running through the conversations like an undercurrent.

Every interaction held potential for betrayal, every smile possibly hiding threats veiled in kindness. There was a reason she had to be here; each person amassed in this ballroom could either hide pieces of truth or horrific lies.

As she moved towards the open bar, the strains of a string quartet filled the air, weaving an almost hypnotic charm around the room. Elena ordered a sparkling water, wanting to maintain a clear mind amid the intoxicating atmosphere that prompted others to drown their secrets in high-priced cocktails. As she turned, a glimpse of movement caught her eye; a man stood by the crowd, isolating himself from the social chatter.

He wore an impeccably tailored suit that emphasized his broad shoulders, and his hair was slicked back with deliberate precision, as if he had just stepped out of a corporate office rather than an upscale gala. There was a caution in his steely gaze, one that echoed the unease Elena felt coursing through the gathering. She noted the way he casually surveyed the room, seeming to measure not just the room's affluent attendees but the elements of danger lurking in their conversations.

With a new purpose, she glided toward him, her instincts igniting. "Aren't you a far cry from the usual crowd?" she inquired with a playful lilt, sound sweetened for allure. Those eyes shifted toward her, narrowing slightly, analyzing her in return.

"And you are quite the anomaly as well," he countered, his voice a low murmur that barely reached her ears. "What brings you to a place where secrets breathe and thrive?"

Elena smiled, feigning innocence. "Perhaps I seek inspiration. Or truth, if I can find it in a place like this."

His lips quirked at the corners. "Truth, in this bubble of deceit? Well, it's brave of you."

"And you?" she asked, echoing his inquiry, darting her gaze between his immediate surroundings to assess his motives. "What keeps you at arm's length?"

There was a flicker of something—perhaps surprise, perhaps recognition—before he glanced around subtly, as though sharing a hidden language with his surroundings. "Some of us prefer the shadows, where truth is less decorative and far less polite."

Elena felt the tension in his words, thick and compelling, drawing her deeper. "Then perhaps we should explore those shadows together?"

His brow raised slightly, an unblinking gaze locked onto hers. After a long pause, his lips formed a sly smile, a devilish contrast to the surface charm surrounding them. "Are you certain you're ready for the truth?"

The challenge in his words stirred her curiosity. "In this city of illusions, what better way to navigate than by discovering the hidden layers of truth?"

Before he could respond, an excited chatter erupted nearby, drawing away attention momentarily. Elena seized the opportunity to press further. "Are you truly intrigued by the truth, or is that simply the mask you choose in this charade?"

His smile vanished as if drawn not by its own accord. "Let's just say I've had my share of revelations and deceptions. There's a method to the madness, and sometimes it leads one astray."

Elena's pulse quickened. Here lay a potential ally—or perhaps even a source of conflict. Yet his ambiguity was intriguing, and she wondered how much he knew about the missing socialite and the tangled webs that bound the elite together. She took a cautious step closer, slicing through the gauzy veil surrounding them.

"What's your name?" she inquired, the risk in her tone sweetened with a hint of inquiry.

The man regarded her thoughtfully. "Call me Gabriel. But remember, names can be deceiving."

As she extended her hand, allowing their fingers to brush, a pulse of electric connection surged through her. For a fleeting moment, the music swayed in the background, the laughter quieted, and all that remained was the tension of their fragile interaction.

"I could use all the help I can get, Gabriel. The world here thrives on whispers, and whispers lead to truths," she offered, her voice steady yet bold.

"But who do you trust within those whispers?" he countered, a flicker of the dangerous edge seeping into his words. "Trust, after all, can be a weapon as sharp as any dagger."

She met the intensity of his gaze, battling with her instincts, sensing a vulnerability beneath his polished coolness. But before she could respond, Vivienne swooped in again, breaking the moment unceremoniously.

"Darling, have you met Gabriel?" Vivienne's bright voice chimed, her presence effortlessly commanding the space. "Quite the man to know in this den of duplicitousness, though I caution—trust can be as elusive as the gowns slip from these ladies' shoulders at midnight."

Elena's heart raced, her thoughts colliding in confusion. Was Vivienne protecting her or warning her against Gabriel? The cunning undertone in her voice peered straight into Elena's core.

Gabriel merely smiled, the charm returning like a mask. "Hope you don't mind a bit of competition, Vivienne. After all, appearances dictate alliances—but they do not always guarantee loyalty."

Elena recalled the frantic warnings, a storm brewing within the vibrant chaos. As she glanced around, she realized every interaction dripped with motives concealed behind extravagant makeup and designer attire, each individual drawn into a dance that could spiral into chaos at a moment's notice.

It was then she understood the gala was not merely a celebration of wealth but a playground for deception where every smile concealed dark truths, whispers wound through delicate fingers like threads of silk, playing a game that could bend lives and shatter trust to pieces.

With each breath, Elena anchored herself to her purpose, observing, probing, and collecting fragments of truth hidden beneath layers of deception. For within this glistening facade, the shadows waited, golden illusions masking claustrophobic darkness.

As the night wore on, Elena melted back into the crowd, her senses heightened, acutely aware of the beat of the night intoxicating the atmosphere—a pulsating rhythm that intertwined fate and desire, weaving stories yet to be told, lives yet to be unraveled. Every conversation echoed, laced with intention, making her more resolute in her need for the truth.

A crystal flute of champagne, garlanded with golden bubbles, slipped into her grasp as she lingered near the edges. The sharp bite of effervescence filled her senses, wrapping her in a plush warmth that disarmed her caution momentarily. Yet deep within, her resolve solidified; there was a delicate equilibrium between attraction and danger in this masquerade, and every decision held weight.

As the evening settled like a blanket, Elena drifted through shimmering clusters of socialite cliques, veiled secrets lurking in conversation—each layered exchange feeding her determination.

She gleaned bits and pieces from conversations; whispers of envy tangled with glimmers of admiration, each completed with thinly veiled threats half-hidden behind laughter and clinking glasses.

"Did you hear about the Turner estate?" one woman exclaimed, her voice filled with feigned innocence. "I hear it's being sold under strange circumstances—such a pity for the lovely inside."

Another lady chimed in, her tone filled with faux warmth. "The owner seems too distracted by the frivolity of parties lately... what with the disappearances."

Elena's pulse quickened at the mention of disappearance. She edged closer, catching snippets of unraveling tales amidst all the pretense.

"It's all in the family... whispers say it's more than just financial ruin."

"True enough. Some families have dark histories that linger, resurfacing like shadows against the light. At this level... nothing is merely coincidence."

Each revelation begged for deeper pursuit, the burden of the evening's tension threading hope and doubt tightly together. Would the glittering facade unravel under the probing light of truth?

As the night mingled on, Elena felt her defenses grow sharper, her instincts honed by each gathered insight. The ballroom felt like a labyrinth of deceit, every turn revealing fissures in the seemingly flawless facade. She was armed with a purpose—and it was time to dig deeper into this society cloaked in glittering facades, each surface shining yet concealing a constellation of darkness hidden beneath.

With a heart steeled against the artifacts of affluence and a mind focused on the mission, Elena slipped deeper into the maze of tales told through glimmering charm, forging a path toward the truth shimmering just below the surface, waiting in the hazy, misrepresented darkness of the elite's dazzling extravagance.

Conversations in the Shadows

The grand ballroom of the Regency Hotel buzzed with laughter, the air thick with a perfume of wealth and ambition. Crystal chandeliers hung like ornate constellations above, refracting light onto a sea of silk and satin. Elena Rourke stood at the edge, a glass of champagne in hand, her gaze sweeping the oscillating crowd of the city's elite. Each face glimmered in an ethereal glow under the extravagant lighting, but behind the polished exteriors, she sensed a grotesque tapestry of deceit and intrigue waiting to unravel.

With a practiced smile, she maneuvered through clusters of conversations, her instincts honed from years of experience as a private investigator. She had entered this world not just to gather information about the missing socialite, but to unearth the covert judgments lurking behind every stately laugh and carefully maintained facade.

"Ah, Elena! You're looking lovely as ever," a voice chimed from her left. It belonged to Jennifer Cartwright, a notorious social climber known for her connections to high-profile politicians and wealthy tycoons. Jennifer's smile was as bright as the sequins sewn into her gown, but her eyes flickered with a predatory glint.

"Thank you, Jennifer. You know how to flatter." Elena took a sip from her glass, the bubbles tickling her nose. "How's your gallery doing? I hear you've landed some big names."

Jennifer surged forward, her enthusiasm palpable. "Oh, it's positively marvelous! We're hosting a charity auction next month, with exclusive pieces from the artist of the hour—Derek Frost. You must come! It's going to be quite the spectacle."

"Wouldn't miss it," Elena replied, keeping her tone light, though her inner skepticism churned. Jennifer had a way of turning every conversation into a sales pitch, masking her ulterior motives beneath a veneer of friendliness.

"By the way," Jennifer lowered her voice, leaning in conspiratorially. "Have you heard any whispers about the McAllister case? Such scandal! I can't imagine the pressure on you."

Elena inclined her head, maintaining an air of intrigue while calculating her response. "Whispers are an inevitable part of the job, Jennifer. But I wouldn't trade my professional secrets for any gossipy tidbit."

"Oh, darling, we both know secrets have a way of finding their way into the light," she replied smoothly. "It's just the nature of this elusive social environment. We're all hiding something, aren't we?"

Another guest interjected, a taller man with slicked-back hair and a designer tuxedo. "Spoken like someone who's seen more than they should," he remarked, his tone mingling camaraderie with irritation. The man was Gregory Hale, a financier with a reputation for brutal business tactics. He leaned towards Jennifer, one eyebrow raised, drawing Elena into an unexpected spat.

"Isn't that right, Jennifer? All this talk of scandal—rather convenient for boosting your gallery's profile, wouldn't you say?"

Jennifer's smile faltered for a fleeting moment, but she quickly regained her composure. "Gregory, do watch your tongue," she chided lightly, her laugh sounding a little too forced. "Just be careful not to trip over your own inflated ego."

Elena watched the interplay, intrigued by this dance of transparency and ambiguity. While Gregory exuded an aura of confidence, she sensed insecurity lurking beneath his well-practiced charm.

"Some may say ego keeps one grounded," he replied smoothly, "but I truly prefer the thrill of the ascent. Do you not agree, Elena?"

With a neutral smile, Elena took another sip of champagne, choosing her words carefully. "Perhaps, but I think it's the shadows that make the light worth chasing." In that moment, she felt the weight of their eyes on her as their laughter dwindled into contemplative silence.

The silence slipped by like a shadow, pregnant with the unspoken truths they all harbored. The tension was simply a reminder that in this space, where laughter echoed around them, nothing was ever as it seemed.

"Bravo," Jennifer finally responded, breaking the unsteady quiet. "I love the poetic flair, Elena! But do keep in mind, while you're admiring the shadows, some of us must navigate through them."

"Or create our own," Gregory added smoothly, fixing his gaze on Elena as if challenging her to engage further or retreat.

Elena decided to push a little deeper. "Navigating through shadows, indeed. I find it fascinating how the heart of this city's elite seems to thrive on getting a little lost. One moment's misstep could send you spiraling into the depths."

Another laugh escaped Jennifer's lips, but it felt harsher this time.

"A risk we all take, I suppose! But isn't it just marvelous how those missteps can be forgotten? Money and charm have a way of erasing sins, darling."

"Maybe," Elena mused, the depths of her gaze unwavering. "But sins have a way of resurfacing, don't they?"

Their expressions flickered; a brief flash of understanding passed between them. In this world of facade, even the subtlest acknowledgment of truth felt daunting. Elena savored that transient moment, feeling that they too—despite their layering deception—could sense the weight of reality creeping at their edges.

The distant toll of a bell announced the commencement of a new speech, and the crowd's murmuring transitioned into rapt attention. For a moment, the masks slipped as all eyes turned toward the podium, where a renowned philanthropist prepared to address the attendees.

Elena stepped back, leaning against the bar, pretending to sip absentmindedly at her champagne to regain composure. While the speaker's voice resonated throughout the ballroom, her focus shifted back to the social climbers around her.

Several more guests joined the conversation, creating a swirling vortex of discussions. She observed participants exchange knowing smiles, alliances forming like delicate filaments in a web.

Across the room, Elena noticed a younger woman, her face obscured by a large feathered hat, whispering urgently to an older man who wore an air of authority. Though Elena couldn't make out their words, she sensed the nervous tension radiating from them.

"Do you see that?" she said to Jennifer, tilting her head toward the pair. "Seems like they have a secret worth hiding."

Jennifer followed her gaze, an amused glimmer in her eyes. "Lydia Ainsworth, daughter of Reginald Ainsworth. Quite the socialite—always flitting about with those important enough to elevate her status. But that's nothing new."

"And who is the older man?" Elena pressed, an itch of curiosity unraveling within her.

"Oh, that's Richard Blythe. A bit of a political fixer, perhaps? Rumors suggest he's been in some shady dealings, but then again, who hasn't, really? Lydia seems to think making connections with him could secure her entrance into the higher echelons of society."

Elena watched their interaction closely, intrigued by the desperation in Lydia's demeanor—the way her hands fidgeted at her side and her eyes darted around. What information did she desperately seek? And at what cost?

"Exciting, isn't it?" Jennifer remarked, her voice laced with mock enthusiasm. "But sweetie, forget that! Who's available to dance?"

"Dance?" Elena replied incredulously, her steel-gray eyes narrowed.

"Why not! Just think of the stories you could gather on the floor! The elite shuffle, and who knows who might need a partner?" Jennifer's callous demeanor veiled her keen perception, setting a scenario for yet another opportunity to elicit information while maintaining her illusion.

"Perhaps, but I think I'd rather not get tangled in that particular ballet tonight," Elena countered, a faint smirk appearing. Instead, she strategized her next moves among the guests, taking note of those who wore their masks like badges of honor.

The musician struck a steady rhythm, leading couples into a dance that mirrored the thrum of their lives—a graceful circle that hid dark intentions.

Elena turned her attention back to the socialites, gauging their conversations. Among the uproar, she spotted a gleam of familiarity. And there he was—Derek Frost, the artist she had been searching for. A cluster of admirers surrounded him, reveling in his brilliance. He prided himself on being the tortured artist yet here, he glistened like a celebrity under hot studio lights.

"That's Derek Frost," Jennifer whispered, her voice dropping low as if the name carried a weighted secret. "Rumor has it, he's tied to the missing socialite somehow."

Elena felt an unfamiliar thrill at the mention. "Really?"

"Yes, well, his works have displayed an enigmatic interplay of chaos and beauty. Some speculate the socialite commissioned him for a portrait before her disappearance—a keepsake, you know. But that's just talk. You could ask him yourself."

"Except he's rather popular at the moment, and I doubt keen ears would overlook if I attempted to break through the gusto surrounding him."

"Oh, darling! There's no harm in trying." With agility, Jennifer pushed Elena toward the crowd and without losing her façade, retreated to embrace another social climber standing by a piano, weaving their stories with clever banter.

Elena took a breath, forcing herself to step into the gathering around Derek.

"Derek!" Jennifer's voice rang through the air, momentarily breaking the enchantment of the swirling guests. "Do you have a moment for your biggest admirer?"

Laughter erupted, warm and inviting, as the artist turned, eyes catching the shimmering lights casting his visage in lethal beauty.

"Of course! I'm always thrilled to hear from my muses!" he retorted, unfurling his charm for the guests surrounding him. "What can I do for you?"

She leaned in, and the group exploded with laughter as she launched into a bubbly conversation rich with flattery and veiled inquiries. Elena observed carefully, focusing less on the pleasant exchange and more on Derek's mannerisms, how he evaded questions and swirled vague tales around his artistry.

While curiosity tediously built, Elena spotted various connoisseurs of the night revitalizing their conversations based on bits and pieces of information exchanged. She began nudging subtly into conversations woven into the tapestry of gossip. Each encounter became part of her investigative fabric, meticulously stitched together by the shifting winds of whispers and deceit.

"Do you think it's true about the missing woman?" a thin voice piped up, belonging to a woman in ivory silk who leaned in like a curious cat, having caught wind of one of the many threads circulating around the room. "I heard she was supposed to launch a new campaign before she vanished."

"That's absolutely true," another guest answered, the man's swift nod indicating a false sense of authority. "I was at the gala; she was the talk of the evening. No one knows what happened afterward—just disappeared into thin air."

Elena's ears perked, the investigative instinct already spiraling like smoke in her chest. "And tell me," she interjected, masking her inquisitiveness under a facade of genuine curiosity. "What else did you hear about her?"

"Ah, just the chatter among those who pretend to care. Something about her affairs, I believe," the man shrugged, dismissive, but his eyes glittered with tales waiting to be told.

"But nobody speaks ill of the missing socialite, do they?" Elena pressed, leaning closer to gauge their reactions, emboldened by the validation growing in each voice.

"She might have had her indiscretions," the woman in ivory replied, a sly smile playing on her lips. "But they're all hushed in respectful tones."

"Oh, how very noble of you." Elena managed a thin smile. "But is it possible that those closest to her may have dealt with something darker?"

The crowd shifted, uncomfortable with the veiled accusations, as their camaraderie faltered under the scrutiny of such a provocative inquiry. Therein lay the unbridled truth—the precarious balance of trust shattered by the ice of mistrust.

"None of the like!" the man protested, a hint of indignation creeping into his tone. "How dare you ruin the mystique surrounding her unfortunate exit!"

Though bubbling tensions flared, Elena reveled in the tension forged by the exchanges.

As more guests circulated around her, she sifted through the crowd, depositing hints and questions and absorbing the vibrant yet murky emotions surrounding the socialite's case.

Soon, it became clear—within each toast, each forced smile, layers upon layers danced around raw truths obscured by affable banter.

By weaving through this world of ambition, greed disguised as civility, she gleaned that the echoes of laughter often concealed harrowing realities.

In a particularly intense moment, Elena caught a glimpse of the young Lydia again, her posture tense, fingers fidgeting against her side.

What were those secrets buried among the chuckles? What shadows lingered behind the decision of maintaining falsehoods?

In a peculiar way, her pulses quickened not just from her investigative thread but from the entwined lives enveloped in the shadows—fragile threads unraveling with every exchange. Each conversation, each laughter, was a delicate step into a dance that could sway either toward revelation or obscurity.

As she observed the crowd around her, mingling in between those weighed-down souls burdened with their truths and others deftly masking their façades, she realized that the shadows didn't always hide danger—sometimes, they merely revealed depth.

Elena needed to focus and gather her thoughts correctly, for it was all too easy to be swept up in the intricate play of personalities, each masked by charm yet laden with suspicions. She withdrew, retreating to the bar momentarily to reconvene and reassess.

As she gazed down into her champagne, the effervescence reminded her of the illusions bursting at the seams—each pop surrounding her a chilling reminder of the society's interlaced lives. Each encounter would serve as a piece of the puzzle she would slowly unfurl in her pursuit of the missing socialite, unaware that she too was climbing deeper into the shadows, where every connection could turn into the light of betrayal at any moment.

Raising her glass in a silent toast to the shadows that danced around her, Elena stepped back into the pulsating heart of the gala, ready to embrace the tangle of conversations that awaited, prepared to peel back the layers of deceit, all the while questioning whom she could trust in a society so proficient in crafting lies.

Secrets in the Champagne Flute

The air inside the gala hall was heavy with opulence, each breath imbued with the unmistakable scent of fine champagne and the fragrance of designer perfumes that enveloped the attendees like a luxurious fog. Elena Rourke stood against the backdrop of shimmering chandeliers, the sound of laughter and clinking glasses creating a symphony of high society's carefully curated facade.

As she adjusted her sleek black dress, she felt a faint shimmer of hope course through her—this was the opportunity to extricate valuable clues from the elite she had infiltrated. Unbeknownst to them, she was not merely a guest; she was a predator wading through a sea of prey, ready to uncover the secrets they desperately attempted to conceal.

Elena surveyed the room, her instincts sharpened. The social elite mingled, their conversations deftly shifting from an array of trivial subjects to the veiled threats that veered just beneath the surface. She had been gathering fragments of whispered truths, but tonight, she was convinced something significant was lurking just beyond her reach. A curiosity lit her eyes as she spotted Veronica Kensington—a prominent figure in the social scene—standing at the far side of the room, her laughter a bit too loud, her demeanor too carefree, as if she was overcompensating for something dark hidden beneath her well-polished exterior.

Elena maneuvered through the throngs of elegantly dressed men and women, her senses heightened. Each smile was laced with trickery; every toast, a masked intent. No one in this room understood the cost of their social positions better than she—a world built on deception where alliances shifted like the evening tide.

"Quite the night, isn't it?" came a voice, smooth and alluring.

Elena turned to find herself face-to-face with Marcello, the dapper entrepreneur whose charm had earned him both admirers and enemies. He tilted his head slightly, a knowing grin etched across his face, as if he held secrets just out of her grasp.

"Are you enjoying the festivities?" he continued, eyes glinting with mischief.

"More than I expected," Elena replied, feigning indifference while her mind raced with thoughts of how to pivot the conversation towards Veronica.

"I can't blame you," he said, moving closer, lowering his voice as if sharing a valuable coin of knowledge. "But don't you find it amusing how artfully crafted these gatherings are? Beauty concealing turmoil, wouldn't you agree?"

Elena met his gaze, assessing him for any ulterior motives hidden behind that smile. "Indeed. This place teems with illusion. One slip, and the whole house of cards could tumble." A subtle challenge hung between them, and she watched as his smile wavered, then returned.

"Well, I wouldn't want to be the one to topple such an edifice. It wouldn't be good for business," he remarked lightly, yet the calculation behind his words didn't escape her.

As he drifted away into the crowd, she turned her focus back to Veronica, who had shifted her position slightly, now holding court with a small group of admirers. Elena decided to take a chance, weaving through the applauding attendees as she made her way closer.

"Veronica!" Elena called, her voice modulating with the rhythm of laughter in the air.

Veronica turned, expression shifting from a façade of delight to genuine surprise as she recognized the investigator. "Elena Rourke! I didn't expect to see a PI here. What an intriguing turn of events!"

"Just following leads," Elena stated, a wolf's smile curling at the corners of her lips. "I hear tonight is rife with connections."

"Connections, indeed!" Veronica echoed, her eyes darting about as if weighing the depth of her words before she continued. "After all, we all have our little secrets to guard, don't we?"

Elena leaned in, her voice low, deliberately conspiratorial. "And what might yours be, Veronica?"

The socialite's laugh vibrated with a mix of mirth and discomfort. "Oh, darling, if I shared with you the thrilling truth of my existence, I wouldn't have anything left to intrigue the masses."

The careful dance of their banter intrigued Elena, and she planned to guide it further.

"Is it true what they say?" Elena ventured boldly, lowering her voice. "That not everyone in your circle is as innocent as they appear?"

There it was—the flicker of uncertainty in Veronica's eyes, the rapid blink before she composed herself. "This is all just harmless fun, Elena. You know the media loves a good story. If I were to pay heed to every rumor, I'd never leave the house."

Under the subtle swirl of champagne splashes and laughter, a darkness lurked—a shadow she hoped to drag into the light. "But the stories can become deadly, can't they?"

That caught Veronica off guard. She stiffened just slightly. "Careful, dear. You never know who might be listening."

Elena felt the weight of that warning; an unvoiced challenge. She knew the socialite had something to hide, and her guarded responses only fanned the flames of Elena's curiosity.

"Believe me, I'm good at keeping my ears open. Secrets have a way of bubbling to the surface at the right moments," Elena remarked, her tone steeped in intrigue. "Tell me, did you hear about the socialite that went missing?"

Veronica's posture shifted, her composure returning. "So many ladies wandering away in search of adventure," she responded, the practiced nonchalance evident in her tone.

Elena leaned in a fraction closer, the noise fading slightly as she whispered, "But what if that adventure turned perilous? What if someone knew more than they let on?"

There was a pause, the tension palpable as sounds blurred around them. For a brief moment, Elena thought she had managed to draw something out of Veronica, something revealing, but then she caught sight of a figure near the bar.

A man in a sharp tuxedo leaned casually, his eyes observing them intently. The fleeting glimpse of familiarity struck her.

"Excuse me, I just spotted someone I need to speak with. I'll catch up with you later!" she declared, darting away before Veronica could protest.

Elena approached the bar, heart racing as she flagged the bartender for another drink—her nerves mounting. She wanted to return to that conversation in the corner with Veronica, where she sensed unchained emotions flickering beneath the polished exterior.

As she downed the fresh glass of champagne, Elena's focus remained on the man she had seen earlier. He appeared out of place, the way he watched her and the interaction with Veronica like a hawk tracking its prey.

"Tom," she greeted confidently, gleaning his name from memory, the corrupt politician's former aide.

"Nice to see you again, Elena," he replied, his smirk playful. "Enjoying the festivities?"

"I hear the crowd has plenty to whisper about. Care to share what you've heard?"

He laughed, as if sharing inside jokes. "Oh, wouldn't you like that? But secrets are best kept among friends."

"Latest scoop on the Kensington girl? I hear she can spin quite the web. I wonder if it's facing a little turbulence?"

"Interesting that you should say that," he replied, taking a step closer, leaning in just enough for their words not to breach the other glowing conversations. "I've heard rumors about her, whispers floating on the breeze."

"Whispers? Funny, isn't it? They say that the highly polished people are scarier than the rough edges."

Tom's grin faded slightly, the amusement edged with caution. "Aren't we all just scraping to stay above it all, Elena? Some of us just have a better view from the top."

"Funny you should say that. I think there are clearer lines of sight from the bottom," she shot back, disengaging from the banter, focusing on an opening. "Like the missing socialite. What do you know about her disappearance?"

Tom hesitated, his expression shifting ever so slightly—uncertainty cracking his confident veneer. "As far as anyone knows, she vanished without a trace. Too many pairs of eyes watching."

Elena sensed the uncut tension between them. The transactional relationship between the elite danced on a perilous line—the consequences profound. She took another sip of champagne, allowing the bubbles to settle in her throat, while scanning the room from the peripheral.

"I do hope the socialite is just playing a tricky game of hide and seek," Elena mused, observing precisely as Tom's eye caught onto something—or someone.

"Far more sinister than that, I'm afraid," he whispered, his demeanor quickly slipping back into cautious air. "I wouldn't poke around too much, Rourke."

Elena's curiosity piqued, she inquired, "What do you mean?"

His gaze slid around, confirming her fears that someone could be listening, thoughts racing behind such a cloth of casual indifference. "Just know fragile alliances crumble quickly. You delve deeper, and it might bite back."

Seizing the moment, she pressed, oblivious to the hidden ramifications swirling in the back of her mind.

"I trust your advice, but I'm driven; the truth has a way of flying back into the light."

"Truth. Lies. All tangled together," he replied cryptically. "This whole scene is a champagne flute filled with shadows—delightfully deceptive."

A shadow flickered past her as she processed his words, her instincts keen. Were his warnings genuine? Or yet another layer in a cocktail of lies?

As she turned to reply, a brief surge of exclamation ignited the air, laughter bursting forth, a toast ringing out, blending the sound of clinking glasses with her racing heart. It was then Elena caught the edge of a whispered conversation drifting toward her. She leaned closer, as the two socialites in black satin gowns conversed just behind her without a hint of awareness—they too, caught up in the world of secrets.

"Did you hear what happened to that poor girl? It's said she was tangled in something... more than just a frivolous affair," one whispered with breathless excitement.

"You can't be serious?" the other gasped, eyes widening with shock. "What do you mean?"

"Rumors say it was violent—something hidden beneath the glamour, something desperate!"

Elena held her breath, her mind racing.

"Of course, everyone will deny it," the first continued. "But you know how these things work—there's always layers. Trust is just an illusion."

"It's not just whispers. A friend saw her in the company of someone notorious just days before she disappeared," the other cautioned. "You should know that some riches come at a price."

What they revealed sent a shiver down her spine. The gears in Elena's mind that had long been turning began to spin faster, conjuring connections, bringing pieces of the puzzle to the forefront, revealing something she already suspected—a thread she needed to pull.

"Who? Who was she with?" Elena wanted to shout, but she restrained herself as the women moved away, their laughter still cascading over her like a veil, keeping her in the shadows.

With her heart pounding fiercely against her chest at the thought of nearing the truth, she would need to act now—to find out about that acquaintance and uncover the name that lingered in the air among the elite.

Elena stepped back into the buoyant ballroom, forcing her breath to steady, feeling the lingering buzz of the champagne upon her tongue. This was it: the revelation she needed, now tantalizingly close.

Just then, she caught sight of a figure weaving through the throngs—a man with sharp features and a crooked smile who clutched a glass of champagne too tightly, as if it soothed some invisible wound. It was Luca Verdi, the renowned artist known as much for his lavish parties as for his scandalous affairs with beautiful socialites.

"Luca!" she called, asserting herself above the ambient noise of the gala.

He pivoted, his expression morphing from light-headed revelry to mild surprise. "Elena! What a delightful surprise. You don't strike me as the gala type."

"Surprises seem to be the theme tonight," she replied, her eyes narrowing slightly. "I need to talk."

His playful grin never faltered, but the glint of apprehension flickered at the edges of his eyes. "Always a pleasure to chat with the great investigator. But not here. Too many ears," he whispered conspiratorially.

Elena nodded, her curiosity about the socialite gnawing at her like a wolf at a weakened prey. "Let's find somewhere quieter then."

He gestured towards a side entrance leading to a dimly lit corridor shadowed by rich velvet drapes, away from the prying eyes of their gilded counterparts.

"Your gallery is still in fashion, I presume?" she asked casually as they stepped deeper into the shadows.

Luca leaned against the wall, his demeanor shifting into that of a wary confidant. "It is, but I prefer to paint the untold stories—the ones ignored by society."

"Like those of the missing socialite?" she probed, her voice low, anchoring him in that fleeting moment of truth.

His expression hardened, and Elena noticed his hand tighten around the champagne flute. "There are many tales in this world that go untold for good reason," he replied carefully.

"Tell me something, Luca. Are you familiar with who she was last seen with?"

"No," he blurted out too quickly, his gaze faltering just a moment before he collected his composure again. "The world of beauty has its shadows. We all wear masks, even the ones who claim to unveil them."

"Then why does it seem you're holding onto secrets of your own?" Elena pressed, taking a small step closer, her voice imbued with palpable intensity.

"Because the truth often comes with a price. At times, silence is preferred."

An electric moment of hesitation hung in the air. "What happened that night, Luca? Someone needs to know," she pressed again, unwavering.

"I do only what the brush teaches me." His expression softened, but it was too late; the thrill of a passing moment had slipped into something far darker behind his darkening gaze. "But perhaps this time, shadows need to stay shrouded."

With that, the fragile edifice of truth began to crack, and as the moments bled into silence, the weight of tightly woven connections teased at the fabric of their world while Elena prepared herself to engulf the consequences.

"Then it's almost too late, isn't it?" she murmured fiercely. The quiet fortitude chilled the air. "Just know, secrets—like those of the champagne flute—will always find a way to spill."

Luca hesitated, eyes narrowing, arms crossed. The game was shifting again, bubbling towards a heady mix of consequences that no one would escape.

As the kaleidoscope of laughter reverberated throughout the gala beyond their curtained refuge, Elena felt the heat spiral within her chest, enthusiasm unbound as her mission surged forward.

Before she could stop herself, she shot out the final challenge, her words colliding with the tension, whispering into the space between them. "How long will you keep yourself in these shadows, Luca? How long until you break?"

The curtain for truth had been drawn; the stage was set for something indefinably remarkable that would unfold in this high-stakes game.

And thus, balled tightly within her grip, Elena was ready to lace their interconnected fates, a step further towards the truth—the moment when all of society's lies began to unravel.

Broken Portraits

In the Artist's Studio

The low hum of the city faded into silence as Elena Rourke stepped into the dimly lit studio, the threshold between the bustling life outside and the shadowed refuge within. A scent of turpentine and unvarnished wood enveloped her, mingling with the musty aroma of canvas and paint. The only light came from a single bulb swinging precariously from the ceiling, revealing the chaotic charm of the space.

Surrounding her were vibrant canvases, each one a window into the artist's soul. Swirls and strokes of color told stories of despair and beauty interwoven in a chaotic dance. Some pieces were bold and chaotic, melding shades of crimson and midnight blue into jagged shapes that spoke of anguish, while others were ethereal, capturing fleeting moments of joy—a glimmer of sunlight breaking through a tree canopy, a fleeting smile. Here, amid the clash of emotions exposed on the canvas, Elena caught glimpses of her own turbulent heart.

She walked deeper into the studio, the cool wooden floor creaking beneath her weight as her eyes roamed over the canvases. Each piece absorbed her—a cacophony of feelings echoed from their depths. One painting in particular caught her breath—a fragmented figure, caught between brightness and shadow, lips parted as if in a silent scream. She felt the weight of that expression, a mirror reflecting her inner chaos as she navigated the labyrinth of her investigation.

"Beautiful, isn't it?" a voice startled her, drawing her attention from the canvas.

Turning, she found the artist standing there, his silhouette etched against the dim light. He was unkempt—hair tousled, eyes shadowed with exhaustion, yet there was a flicker of intensity about him that sparked her curiosity. He wore a paint-stained smock that hung loosely on his frame.

"Beautiful?" she echoed, her voice heavy with contemplation. "Or haunting?"

"Is there a difference?" he replied, stepping closer, his gaze piercing through the dimness like a lighthouse beam through fog. "Art is the chaos of life."

Elena nodded, taking a moment to absorb his words. The artist's passion vibrated in the air, intertwining with her own restless heart. "You seem to have captured something profound here. It feels…" she hesitated, "personal."

His lips quirked into a wry smile. "Everything is personal, isn't it?

It's how we cope. This painting," he gestured to the anguished figure, "was born from pain. I guess we all wear our stories on our sleeves, or in my case, on canvas."

"I understand that feeling all too well." Elena stepped further into the studio, her fingertips brushing against the rough texture of another canvas. "I'm looking for someone—someone who seems to have been swallowed whole by this city."

"Another canvas for your collection, I presume?" he asked, his voice laced with irony.

"A missing socialite," she replied, meeting his gaze. "Spirited away, just like the colors in these paintings."

The artist's expression shifted, a flicker of recognition sparking in his eyes. "People often disappear into their own darkness," he said softly, "whether visibly or invisibly." He paused, contemplating her words. "What do you know?"

"More than I hoped," she admitted, glancing back at the fragmented figure as though it held the secrets she sought. "But nothing is as straightforward as it seems."

"Welcome to life." The artist stepped closer, the tension between them thickening like the paint drying on his canvases. "What if I told you that each brushstroke carries a weight? That every choice can either bind us together or tear us apart?"

"I'd believe you," she said, suddenly aware of how much she wanted to understand him. There was a rawness about him that drew her in—had she not spent years piecing together lives from shards of fractured truths?

"Come," he said, beckoning her to follow him as he moved further into his sanctuary of creativity. The back wall was adorned with a collection of smaller pieces—sketches and studies that had paved the way for his refined works. "Sit," he gestured to a low stool among the scattered paint tubes and brushes, his movements fluid, taking on the grace of an artist at home within his world.

A soft sigh escaped her as she settled, her weary body momentarily cradled in the embrace of his chaotic realm. "Tell me about this one."

She pointed to a smaller canvas, an abstract portrayal of a woman with flowing hair, caught in a moment of ecstatic rigidity. The woman's arms were raised as if reaching for something just beyond her grasp, a wistful yearning embedded in every stroke.

"Ah," the artist's voice took on a low richness, drawing out the story nestled within the strokes. "That piece was inspired by a woman caught between two lives—one of obligation and another of desire. She was my muse for a time, but you know how muse relationships can be. Fleeting, like shadows in the night."

"Like the socialite?" Elena leaned in, intrigued. "What was she like?"

"The socialite?" he echoed, his brow furrowing. "She was… captivating. Everyone adored her, and she had dreams painted in hues that were almost too bright for anyone to touch. But she was also a tempest, full of secrets layered like the paint on my canvases."

"Did you know her well?" Elena took a mental note of his tone, sharp yet tinged with longing.

"I thought I did," he replied, looking away, the shadows of memories passing over his features. "But people are like portraits—they can hide unimagined worlds behind a seemingly perfect facade."

"And behind those facades lie pain and grief, right?" Elena's voice felt fragile, yet firm, as if prodding at an open wound.

"Yes," he said, the weight of that admission heavy in the air. "Art allows us to explore those depths without losing our souls entirely. The pain spills outward, and sometimes we catch glimpses of our truths."

"Does it help?" she prompted quietly, intrigued.

"Help?" He laughed softly, a sound tinged with melancholy. "Art is a double-edged sword. It heals and it wounds. I pour everything in, every drop of anguish, and somehow, it transforms into beauty. But with it comes a reminder of what we've sacrificed to create."

"I can relate to that." Elena felt an undeniable kinship with him, memories swirling like echoes in her mind, of moments spent untangling the webs of lives shattered by both choices and circumstance. "I've sacrificed a lot trying to find the truth."

"When you seek truth," he said thoughtfully, "it often leads you into the depths of someone else's darkness. Every revelation comes at a price."

"Is that what happened with her? The socialite?"

He nodded slowly, the light in his eyes dimming. "She was in search of her own truth, just like all of us. And then she vanished, taking all those layers of secrets with her. People may claim to know her, but none truly touched her heart. The world celebrated her shape, not her essence."

The words hung in the air between them like the scent of oil paint, thick and consuming. Elena could feel that she was peeling back layers, both of the artist and the socialite, revealing raw emotions behind every façade.

"Do you think someone hurt her?" she asked, her heart pounding as she navigated the fragile territory of their conversation.

His eyes darkened. "Those in her world often mistake ambition for love. They play dangerous games for power and influence—beneath the glitzy surface, they are ready to devour anyone who crosses the line."

"You paint a haunting picture," she said, her voice barely above a whisper.

"Art often reflects what exists beneath the skin. Look closely, and you'll find the grief entwined within," he gestured to the canvases, gesturing toward unblemished spaces that became voids.

As a wave of urgency surged within her, Elena leaned forward, wanting to grasp every ounce of his insight. "What if I told you that I found something connected to her—a bracelet she wore? They say it was hers, a connection to the heart of it all."

The artist's brow arched, curiosity flickering in his gaze. "What kind of bracelet?"

"It was delicate, beautiful," she described, feeling the weight of its memory in her hands. "A piece of her history, I believe."

He pondered her words, then nodded knowingly, his chest rising and falling with each breath. "Perhaps her heart was less defined by the clutches of society and more by threads of intimacy interwoven in art. Sometimes, beauty is the very thing that invites danger."

"Have you ever painted someone without truly knowing them?" Elena asked not just of him but of herself as well. She was interrogating the instinct that had pulled her into this investigation, the feeling that something deeper was hidden beneath her desire to unearth the mystery surrounding the missing woman.

"Every day," he confessed, vulnerability surfacing in his voice. "We all wear masks. I send each canvas out into the world, naked yet clothed in colors, emotions in their purest forms. But no one really sees me or the real story. They see what I show them. Perhaps, that's the tragedy."

"Perhaps that's why I'm here," Elena mused, wondering if she, too, had become an artist in her own right, painting stories through inquiry and investigation. "Searching for truth amid layers of deception."

As the moment drew heavy with emotion, silence settled between them, punctuated only by the sound of a paintbrush being dipped into dark pigments.

"Will you allow me to paint you?" he asked suddenly, his voice low and earnest. "My canvas needs your story, a fragment of truth bleeding into the art I've yet to create. You bring light into dim corners, and I want to capture that."

Elena hesitated, torn between the offer and what it meant—a step into intimacy that felt both thrilling and terrifying. "What would you want me to do?"

"Just sit still and let me reveal the layers buried beneath your skin. Tell me about your story, your struggles." He moved closer now, his breath warm against her face. "Whatever you feel, allow it to emerge into the open."

The intimacy of the proposition ignited a whirlwind of emotions within her. Vulnerability and the promise of revelation danced on the tips of her thoughts. She could feel a storm of words bubbling up inside her, yearning to be released. He had seen through her battle scars; would sharing her truths free her from them?

"Alright," she said finally, a rush of acceptance carrying her voice. "But remember, art is deceiving. You may think you know me, but I promise, I wear many masks."

"Good," he smiled, a genuine warmth radiating as he stepped away from her, giving her space, allowing the moment to settle. "Masks can be as beautiful as the faces beneath them. It's those layers I want to reveal."

She watched as he prepared, her heart pounding with the anticipation of bare honesty. The dim light flickered as he set up his easel, carefully selecting colors that spoke to him—each tube a small universe of emotion that he coaxed into being.

"Tell me," he said, his brush poised above the canvas, "since the socialite entwines through your investigation, what do you see in this world?"

Elena inhaled sharply, the question reopening her own wounds, fractures through which the sunlight had forgotten to trespass. "I see a world filled with masks, a dance of shadows and light. I see ambition cloaked in charm, but also vulnerability—their scars reflect the scars on me."

"Then let those layers emerge," he said, looking at her intently. "Let them breathe on the canvas."

With that, Elena let her memories spill forth—stories she had buried under the rubble of her resolve. She told him of sleepless nights spent unraveling threads of deceit, shared fears of losing herself within the spirals of darkness, and how even the drive for truth felt like a specter hunting her.

As she spoke, he translated her stories into strokes of paint, merging emotion with artistry. Each whisper carved into the canvas brought a new understanding—a visceral connection binding them through shared experience. He poured his heart into his art, fulfilling both his yearning and the longings filling her. The studio transformed into a cocoon, the air pulsing with the heartbeat of their revelations.

Hours melted away in this sacred exchange, the artist weaving vibrant colors into the canvas as Elena poured out herself, each confession a brushstroke aligning her truths and heartaches. They exchanged laughter and sorrow—the duality of human experience echoed between them, merging like oil and water.

Finally, as the final licks of paint dried, he stepped back, analyzing the artwork. It resided not just as a likeness but as a testament to their intertwined vulnerabilities.

"It's…alive," he said softly, awe threading into his words. "You'll see your soul in every layer."

"What does it say?" Her voice trembled with anticipation.

"It says you are more than the sum of your fears, that you dare to navigate through chaos, seeking not just answers but embracing your own journey."

Elena felt the tide rise within her, an overwhelming wave of gratitude. "Thank you," she whispered, her heart swelling with emotion.

"No, thank you," he replied, a sincerity woven through his tone. "For trusting me enough to reveal your essence. This moment—right here—reminds me that we are all stitching together our truths, one brushstroke at a time."

As Elena stepped closer to the canvas, seeing both her struggles and her strength depicted, a sense of liberation washed over her. Art had become the vessel through which they dared to confront their truths, stitching together their individual scars into a shared tapestry of emotion.

Little did they know, the connection forged in the dimly lit studio would ripple through the storm ahead, entangling their lives further in the web of deception awaiting them.

They may have embraced their vulnerabilities in that sacred moment, but beyond the warm glow of the studio, outside of this protective space, danger loomed—shadows gathering at the edges of their truth-filled exchange, just waiting to spill back into the world.

Art as Exorcism

The dim light of the artist's studio cast cryptic shadows across the bare walls, hinting at the untold stories that lingered in the air. Canvases, both completed and in progress, lined the room, their painted surfaces a chaotic blend of vibrant colors and dark hues, much like the artist's soul. Elena Rourke stepped inside, her heart racing with curiosity and trepidation. This was the sanctuary of a man who captured the essence of anguish, a place where art was born from pain and despair.

The artist, a tall man with a mane of wild, untamed hair, stood in front of an easel, his eyes glazed over with concentration. He stepped back momentarily to scrutinize the waves of color swirling on the canvas before him—a tempest of emotion that seemed eerily alive.

"Can I help you?" he asked, breaking the silence that enveloped them. His voice was rasped, as if he had just emerged from under the weight of his own solitude. A faint smudge of paint adorned his cheek, making him seem like a poet torn from time, a tortured spirit seeking solace through strokes of genius.

Elena hesitated, taking in the cluttered room, the scent of turpentine melding with the dust of forgotten dreams. "I'm looking for answers about the socialite who disappeared. I heard you knew her. I thought... I thought maybe your art holds some truth to her story."

The artist regarded her for a moment, his expression unreadable. Then, surprisingly, he nodded. "You want to know about her through my madness? Art, my dear investigator, is an exorcism. It unpacks the haunting aspects of life, confronting demons that would rather remain hidden."

Elena felt a chill course through her. "Demons?"

He waved a hand across the room, gesturing toward the canvases where vibrant reds met murky blacks, swirling together in a chaotic dance. "Every piece I create is a battle fought within me. Each brushstroke is meant to wrestle with memories that cling like shadows, to purge the specters of regret and grief. This one," he said, pointing towards a hauntingly beautiful canvas of a woman whose face was obscured, "is the embodiment of an unresolved past—much like your missing person."

Elena took a step closer, her breath caught in her throat. The woman on the canvas, with her soft features blurred into a whirl of emotions, echoed the disappearance of the socialite. "It's stunning," she whispered, her fingers aching to reach out and touch the paint.

"Art is my sanctuary, but it also holds the keys to my disdain. You see, she was a muse and a chaos—a fleeting inspiration—but she also trapped me in her whims, upending my world. Submerged in all her grandeur, I lost pieces of myself just as she lost her way." His voice held an edge of bitterness veiled beneath layers of complexity.

Elena felt the heavy weight of his words, a mirror reflecting her own struggles. "What do you mean?"

He turned back to the canvas, a frown creasing his brow. "She represented everything—the beauty, the allure, the intoxicating scent of ambition that filled the air around her. Yet all those around her were slowly drowning, gasping for air while she danced above, oblivious. I wanted to capture her essence, to render her immortal through my work. But the deeper I delved, the more I discovered layers of despair just below the surface."

Elena looked at him, taking in his raw honesty. This wasn't just an artist speaking; it was a man who was grappling with his own failures. "You felt responsible?"

He scoffed lightly, letting out a sad laugh. "Responsible? Perhaps, but it was more than that. I've carried my own demons into the light through her image. Every vibrant stroke is a confession, every dark shadow a reminder of the sadness she inadvertently brought upon everyone she encountered."

Elena was captivated, her investigative instincts igniting like a flame. "What secrets did she carry, then?"

The artist sighed deeply, rubbing the back of his neck as though the weight of memory bore down upon him. "Secrets only the canvas knows. In the beginning, she would come to my studio, and I would create her portrait, capturing her beauty, her sparkle." He paused, searching for the right words.

"But with each stroke, I began to notice the hesitance in her smile. There would be silence between our sessions, moments where she seemed adrift in a sea of confusion. Sometimes, she wouldn't show up at all, and I would wait, wondering if those were signs—a plea for help, or merely the whims of a socialite."

A spark flickered in Elena's mind, igniting her curiosity. "Did she confide in you?"

He shook his head slowly, and Elena could see the struggle etched upon his face. "She was an enigma even to herself—an artist caught in a canvas of frivolity. I tried to reach for her, but it was useless; every attempt was thwarted by the masks she wore. One minute, she'd be dancing in laughter; the next, she'd be lost in thought, a shadow of her former self."

Elena felt the familiar pang of empathy grip her chest, a reflexive response to the struggles of those lost in their desires. "Could you paint her secrets?"

He canted his head slightly and studied her intently. "Can I paint the chaos within the human soul? Perhaps, but only through metaphor. It takes courage to peel away the layers woven into one's identity."

She sensed the challenges he faced, both as an artist and as a man. "Does it hurt?"

"Every time," he replied softly, his voice dropping to a whisper. "Confronting one's demons is like staring into the abyss. It wants to draw you in, to swallow you whole. But like every artist, I've learned to wield my brush as both shield and sword."

With each revelation, Elena could feel the connection building between them, forged in the fires of vulnerability. "What did you learn from her?"

He turned back to the canvas, standing silent for a moment as if the question hung in the air, waiting for him to conjure an answer.

Then, as if compelled by some unseen force, he began speaking again. "She taught me about suffering—its capacity to shape a person, to create beauty for the world to see, yet hide anguish within. I once thought art was merely an avenue for self-expression, but it's an avenue for redemption. Each piece is a testament to struggle—a whisper of hope amid despair."

Elena nodded, her mind racing to comprehend the profound insight housed within his words. "So your art becomes an exorcism?"

The artist's eyes sparkled with weary recognition. "Exactly, Elena. Just as I etch my demons into the fabric of my work, she struggled against her own void, grappling with an identity—being a glamorous socialite on the surface while swimming in insecurity beneath. I believe she was searching for redemption too."

Elena moved closer, mesmerized by the depth of his passion. "Do you think she found it?"

"I wish I could say she did. In our brief moments together, I felt glimpses of desperation. At times, she sought comfort in the arms of admiration, thinking it could fill the void, but I feared it only deepened her isolation." He paused, the intensity of his gaze locking onto hers. "Just like me, she was creating art through her existence, but forgot that shadows love to linger."

A heavy silence wrapped around them, and Elena felt the sting of understanding settle deep within her. "What about love?" she dared to ask, breaking through the weight of their exchanged truths.

He sighed, the tension in his shoulders easing as he laughed softly, a mixture of irony and sorrow. "Love." He spat the word with a hint of venom, staring into the distance.

"Love can be as cruel as it is gentle. It serves as both muse and malevolent spirit, spinning its net while leaving one in tangled, chaotic shadows."

Elena felt her heart ache at his words, recognizing the universal truth in them. "So what do we do then? How do we escape it?"

"By freeing ourselves from the shackles of expectation, the masks that we wear. It is a fight, a constant battle, both in art and in life. We carve out spaces where honesty can breathe, where the pain can be expressed. And sometimes, even that act of expression becomes the very salvation we need."

As he spoke, Elena realized the power their meeting held; it was a tipping point—a collision of souls yearning for resolution. "How do we let go of the darkness?"

He turned towards her, an understanding glint illuminating his eyes. "We don't let it go, Elena. We embrace it like an old friend, allowing it to wash over us, to mingle with our joys and sorrows, to learn from it and grow. Just like brush strokes blending into harmony on the canvas. It's a constant process."

Elena felt a wave of warmth surge within her, a rush of connection binding them together in the tumult of their respective journeys. It was a poignant reminder that healing could exist outside the scars—perhaps, she mused, within the shared act of vulnerability.

"What if art isn't enough?" she whispered, her vulnerability surfacing anew.

"Then we make it enough. We transform our pain into purpose, creating a dialogue that transcends mere survival. I reflect on the socialite by painting, but the action carries weight beyond myself. In our connections, we find the alchemy that frees us from despair."

As they spoke, the darkness inside the room seemed to lift, replaced by a sense of awakening and possibility. Elena realized they were both victims of the shadows, desperately searching for redemption through their art—in their lives.

Her gaze wandered back to the canvases, each piece becoming a window to their truths, mirrors of souls longing to be whole again. "Will you show me more?" she inquired gently, craving to understand this artist, to see not just the artwork, but the essence of pain transformed into something remarkable.

With a slow, deliberate nod, he led her deeper into the studio, the world beyond fading into a realm of human emotion captured in color and form. He whispered stories behind each painting, sharing the stories scrawled in the depths of his heart—the battles fought and won, the losses that carved their way into every brushstroke.

Each canvas harbored fragments of his heart, pieces of his vulnerability woven into the fabric of an artist who had battled relentlessly against the demons within. And as he unveiled the works, sharing his cathartic journey through art, Elena felt a shift in herself, a powerful resonance with her own quest for truth and healing.

Time lost meaning as the dance between artist and investigator continued, exploring the invisible threads binding their stories—a delicate tapestry of pain and redemption spun behind the canvas.

And amid this whirlwind of emotions encased in paint, they began to write a new narrative; one of empathy, connection, and the overwhelming realization that even in the darkest corners, hope could shine brightly, guided by the brush of an artist determined to find light through the shadows.

Buried Truths

It was a rainy evening, droplets cascading down the large glass windows of the art studio, blurring the lines between the outside world and the chaos within. The light was dim, casting a soft glow on the canvases that lined the walls, each one telling its own story of anguish and beauty. The air was heavy with the scent of oil paint, mingled with something darker—the scent of unspoken words, lost corners of the heart begging to be found.

Elena Rourke stood in the middle of the studio, her heart resonating with the thrum of uncertainty echoing in her mind. She had never been one to shy away from complexities, but the layers of emotion unfolding around her threatened to engulf her. The artist, a gaunt figure with a haunted gaze, studied her with a curious blend of apprehension and resolve, as if he held the very keys to the maze that was both his life and hers.

"Why did you want to meet with me?" he asked, his voice a gravelly whisper, as though the act of speaking drained him of strength. "You're the investigator. Surely the painted lines of my existence don't interest you." His skepticism hung in the air, a palpable tension that Elena felt in her bones.

"Because I've learned that every stroke has a story," she replied, her voice steadier than she felt. "And sometimes those stories intertwine in ways we don't expect."

He stepped back, leaning against a nearby easel, his arms crossed defensively. "Stories can be misleading. They're often dressed in pretty colors. You might think you're seeing the truth when it's merely a façade."

Elena's mind raced. She had come seeking answers about the missing socialite, Anna Delacroix, but now her own motivations felt obscured amid the turmoil of the artist's world. "Then let's strip the façade away. Tell me about Anna."

The artist looked away, his gaze drifting towards a particularly striking canvas—a somber portrayal of a woman surrounded by twisted trees and shattered mirrors. The image tugged at her heart, a visceral reminder of fragility, and she felt its weight blend with the heavy atmosphere of the room.

"What do you think you see in her?" he finally responded, his eyes narrowing as he scrutinized her. "You think she was just a socialite, a life of privilege and allure? That she glided through the world effortlessly?"

"No," Elena answered resolutely, drawn into the depths of the mystery. "I don't believe that at all. I think she was hiding."

"More than you can imagine," he said, his voice barely over a whisper. "She was beautiful, yes, but beauty can be a weapon. It can trap you in illusions—both for oneself and for others. If you're not careful, you become merely a reflection of what others see."

The artist stepped toward her, his eyes now fierce, and Elena felt the chill of something deeper lurking beneath the surface of the conversation.

"You think you're after her truth, but your search mirrors your own blind spots. Tell me, Elena, what does it say about you that you feel compelled to find her?"

The question hung heavily in the air, and for a moment, Elena felt exposed under his gaze. She took a breath, grounding herself. Her own shadows were well-known to her—the failures, the losses, the regrets. "I'm a private investigator. It's my job to uncover truths, to bring closure, for the ones left behind. Anna's case isn't just another case; it's my chance to right the wrongs."

"Right the wrongs?" he repeated, an incredulous note in his voice. "Or expose the wrongs? You may find more than you bargained for."

A shiver ran down Elena's spine at the hint of foreboding in his words. She had always approached her cases with resolute determination, but now doubt crept in. "You don't know me."

"No, but I see you," he replied. "And you should know that unveiling her story will not just affect her life; it will unearth old ghosts, perhaps even your own."

Elena shifted uneasily, sensing the truth in his words. She wasn't merely pursuing Anna's truth, but also her own unresolved traumas—her juggling career, her shaky relationships, and her fear of failure. But there was something about the artist—a magnetic pull that drew her closer to him, compelling her to expose the darkness hidden within both of their pasts.

"The layers of Anna's life are not just a canvas," she said quietly, forcing herself to challenge him. "They're entangled with yours and mine. What you know could bridge the gaps of understanding about her."

His expression softened slightly, and he nodded, the tension easing just a fraction. "Anna and I shared a history that tangled the threads of both our lives. But those threads were frayed by denial and repressed truths. She buried parts of herself so deep, it was as if she was trying to erase her own existence."

"Did you love her?" Elena asked, watching as he flinched, his eyes clouding with pain.

"In a way," he replied slowly, visibly grappling with the weight of his feelings. "But my love was not enough to pull her from the storm she created within herself. Being in love with a person so disconnected from their own reality puts you in a paradox of passion and despair."

The artist turned and began to pace, a restlessness emanating from him like a tangible energy. "You see, Anna was more than just the charming socialite displayed at gala events. She was brilliant yet riddled with fears—fears that twisted her soul and made it easier to exist in a facade than confront the chaotic truth of her being."

Elena followed his movements, her instincts urging her to delve deeper. "What kind of fears?"

He hesitated, crossing his arms tighter against his chest as if shielding himself against the world.

"The fear of not being enough, fear of losing her identity in a world that demanded she conform to a role. Inside, she was a tempest, disguising herself with artifice to survive the judgments and harshness of reality."

As she listened, Elena felt echoes of her own struggles ripple within her, and the link between Anna and herself solidified. "And you?" she pressed, taking a step closer. "What about your fears?"

"Mine?" he said abruptly, his demeanor shifting as shadows danced in his eyes. "I was trapped in the allure of who I could be to her, but I lost myself trying to save her."

Elena favored his admission. "And that's where the truth lies, isn't it? Caught in the duality of love and despair. That's what I need to uncover. If I can piece together her story—the real one—maybe I can grasp the truth that has eluded me."

"Truth can sometimes be more dangerous than the secrets we hold," he warned, his voice a dark rumble.

"Maybe," she countered, her resolve strengthening. "But I have to try."

"Fine," he sighed heavily, running a hand through his disheveled hair. "But consider this: dealing with Anna, or confronting your own reality can unearth more than you're prepared for. Her legacy is buried deep, and it won't surface nicely."

Elena braced herself for whatever he was about to divulge. "I'm listening."

He paused, staring at the ground as if searching for the right words hidden within the wooden planks. "We met long before the world saw her as a socialite. In college, she was a student of art—raw talent. We were both naïve, enveloped in dreams. But dreams morphed into artillery for both of us."

"Artillery?" She leaned in, intrigued.

"Yes," he murmured. "Weapons against the judgments of society; tools to carve out realities that were almost too painful to face."

"What made her become that woman?" Elena pressed, urgency ringing in her voice.

"Her rise to socialite and the obsession with the glamorous became both her prison and her art. And in our youth, we swore we'd break away from all that—transform the world through our creativity. But it twisted us both."

"Twist?" Elena's heart raced. "You mean she was drawn into it despite her aversion?"

"Exactly. The allure of acceptance was overpowering for her. Each brushstroke turned into a mask that obliterated her identity. That's where I lost her."

"And you," Elena nudged. "You let her."

"I did," he admitted, a heavy sadness lacing his words. "But it frightened me more. I could see her transformation and tried to pull her back, thinking I could be her anchor. But she swam deeper into the undercurrents of society."

Elena's heart sank. "You were close to her, yet still so far."

He nodded, the realization a painful weight on his shoulders. "And therein lies the irony. We could never save one another. By the time I realized, it was too late."

"Too late?"

"By the time Anna discovered her own rot, her heart had become shackled, chained by what genuine love could mean to her. And when you become bound to a lie, the truth is a bitter enemy."

Silence enveloped the studio, a solemn shroud settling over both of them. Inside, the heartbeat of their shared experience resonated—two souls drifting in unconnected spirals of longing.

"What did you find?"

He raised his gaze sharply, eyes flashing with an urgent fire. "We both found ourselves painted in shades of betrayal, but at different times. She alienated truth to survive the roiling storm in her mind, and I plunged deeper into my own isolation as her shadow."

Elena shifted, the weight of his confession resting heavily between them like an anchor. "Can you forgive her?"

"I stopped blaming her long ago," he replied. "But the ache of unfulfilled potential still lingers. When the truth is buried, it festers. And in our case, it transformed us both."

"When you said her legacy lies deep, what exactly do you mean?" she inquired, sensing there was more to the story.

He hesitated, doodling in the air with a paintbrush he absentmindedly picked up, and a look of concern replaced the thoughtful glaze. "There was something we created together—a piece of art that she never showcased, a dark mirror to her true self. I kept it under wraps, and finally showed it during our last encounter, but it terrified her to see her reality unveiled."

"What was it?"

"A self-portrait of a woman, unmasked. Naked, raw, vulnerable. Not the woman of grace she had become in the public eye."

Elena's eyes widened, grasping the magnitude of what he was revealing. "And? What happened?"

"There was chaos. She saw herself for the first time, detached from the artifice she'd created, and I could see the frenzy unfold behind her eyes. Tears streamed down her face, mixing with shame and denial."

"Was that when she went missing?"

He paled, and the connection between the past and present tightened like a noose. "Yes, that night marked the shift. She fled from herself, from me. I think perhaps the last straw was recognizing how deeply she had buried her truths."

"It's not just about art," Elena pressed, desperation creeping into her voice. "It's about identity, about how we define ourselves versus how the world perceives us."

"Exactly." His voice took on a haunted quality. "And posed in that canvas was everything she feared to acknowledge—a reflection so agonizing it shattered her."

Elena felt the pieces snap into place, the labyrinth of their tangled past began to unfurl before her. "She ran. But she left you a parting gift."

"A gift or a curse?" he murmured, haunted.

"Perhaps both," she said, resonating with his anguish. "And if we can uncover that truth, we may break the cycle—for her and for ourselves."

He turned away again, the colors swirling in delirium reflecting in his eyes. "What if you find nothing but despair?"

"Then we'll face it together. We owe it to her and to ourselves."

The silence stretched, heavy yet filled with unsaid promises, as they began to weave their fraying threads into a new narrative. Together, they would unearth the buried truths, even if it meant traversing the darkest corners of their shared hauntings.

Trust on the Brink

The Political Layer

The first step into the politician's office felt like stepping into a gilded cage. Elena Rourke adjusted her grip on the leather strap of her bag, taking a moment to absorb the opulence surrounding her.

It was a far cry from the gritty back alleys and smoky bars she had frequented during her investigation. The plush harmonies of deep brown woods and marbled accents sang a discordant lullaby to her instincts. Everything about this place screamed power, but she could feel the undercurrent of danger lurking beneath the surface.

The office was bathed in the warm glow of strategically placed chandeliers, their light casting an inviting aura over the lavish furnishings. On one wall, an oversized portrait of the city's mayor hung prominently, framed in gold and exuding confidence. It was a carefully constructed illusion, designed to make visitors feel small and insignificant, as if the very wall of power could consume them. The lavish desk in front of her seemed to dominate the space, cluttered with papers that promised both opportunity and ruin.

Elena stepped further in, her shoes silent against the plush carpet. She caught sight of a figure lounging casually behind the desk, his well-tailored suit a testament to wealth. He appeared every bit the part of the charming politician—sharp features softened by a disarming smile, the kind that could convince anyone that he was on their side. But Elena had learned to see the cracks beneath the surface; this man was a façade, a puppet master with strings that could lead to any number of dark places.

"Ms. Rourke," he said, his voice smooth as honey but edged with an unspoken menace. "I've been hearing quite a bit about your tenacity. It's… commendable."

Elena met his gaze unflinchingly. "I'm just doing my job, Mr. Darnell. The missing socialite has many people concerned. I was hoping you could help clarify a few things."

Darnell leaned back in his chair, steepling his fingers together, his eyes glimmering with amusement. "Help? Ah, that's a loaded term in my world. But let's not beat around the bush. You want to know how a woman like Francesca Thornton could vanish without a trace. You've come to the right place."

His offer hung in the air, heavy with implications. Elena sensed the way he controlled the conversation, steering it like a ship. Here was the artistry of politics in its finest form—words crafted to lure, promises dressed in deception. She held her ground, letting her instincts guide her as she probed for weaknesses.

"What do you mean?" she asked, keeping her voice steady. "You know something, don't you?"

Darnell's smile faltered for a mere second, but it was enough for Elena to recognize the shift. Resentment bubbled beneath his polished surface, and the glint of something far more sinister flashed in his eyes. "I'm just a humble politician, Ms. Rourke. I don't dabble in the affairs of the wealthy elite. They have their own ways of dealing with issues."

"Or lack thereof," she countered, crossing her arms. "If you're not involved, why are you so very interested in her disappearance?"

"I wouldn't say interested," he replied smoothly, gesturing dismissively. "More like concerned with the tide of public opinion. A woman like Francesca represents an image our city cannot afford to lose. Her disappearance sends ripples through the foundations we've worked so hard to build."

Elena studied him carefully, perceiving the delicate layers of trust and deception intertwined like the patterns of fine silk. "You mean to say appearances matter more than the truth?"

Darnell laughed softly, a sound devoid of genuine mirth. "Truth is subjective. What matters is how we shape it." He motioned toward the sprawling skyline visible through the floor-to-ceiling windows. "In this city, my dear, power is an illusion, and those who wield it must navigate through veils of darkness with caution."

As he spoke, Elena's mind whirred with possibilities. The man before her was an opportunist, a serpent cloaked in a gentleman's attire, wielding charm like a weapon. A single misstep could land her in depths of political intrigue she couldn't hope to escape. There were whispers, rumors that brushed against the city's surface, and she was already sinking deeper with each conversation.

"Is that why you moved Francesca into the shadows? Because she was a liability?"

The fiery edge of his voice returned, sliding into an icy calm. "Now, now. Let's not make assumptions, shall we? The elite can be quite protective, especially when something threatens their way of life. It can lead to… unfortunate consequences."

The undertones of threat vibrated in the air, the room suddenly feeling smaller, the weight of his power pressing down on her. Was he asserting his influence or warning her away from knowing too much? This was the thin line she now walked, the fragile tension of her situation transforming into a palpable wave of danger.

Elena needed to tread carefully, abandoning any false sense of security the plush furniture suggested.

"Someone must know something," she pressed. "If Francesca was indeed a liability, wouldn't her friends be worried? It's not like she was the type to disappear without telling anyone."

Darnell waved a hand dismissively, the casual gesture betraying a deeper unease. "People prefer to forget difficult truths, Ms. Rourke. Wealth can insulate you from consequences, but the truth?" He leaned towards her, his voice dropping to a conspiratorial whisper. "It has a way of surfacing when least expected."

It was the flicker of a warning in his tone that caught her attention. Perhaps Darnell was aware of more than he let on. A soft ping inside her mind echoed with premonition; this was a man who feasted upon the secrets of the city—who thrived on the very shadows Elena sought to unearth.

"Let's not get lost in more hearsay," Elena said, the firmness returning to her voice. "What I need is concrete information. I assure you, the missing socialite's friends will be speaking up soon, and should they think you're involved…"

Darnell's expression changed, a flicker of aggression flashing across his normally composed features. "I believe we both understand the stakes at hand, Ms. Rourke. If you go digging too deeply, you might just unearth skeletons that would rather remain buried."

His threat hung in the air, wrapping around them like a shroud. Elena felt the oppressive atmosphere constricting her—full of whispered deals and muted resentments. This was the political layer she had encountered, thick with manipulation seasoned with elements of fear, a landscape where power emerged from darkness, and trust was a currency more valuable than gold.

With that final push, he leaned back, arms relaxed at his sides, inviting her to reconsider her approach.

"Any other inquiries?" he asked with a smirk, his voice returning to that charming lilt, a jester cloaked in a king's robes.

Elena swallowed with difficulty, pushing back against the unease that had settled. She was no pawn in his game, and she refused to let him dictate her pace. "Just one," she replied, a steely determination lining her voice. "Tell me who Francesca was last seen with, and I will consider our conversation finished."

"Ah, that's where it becomes tricky," he replied, feigning contemplation. "But perhaps… you can meet the right people, grasp the threads of the web I spin from my corner office."

His suggestion dangled like bait on a hook. She needed to make a decision. Was it worth pursuing this avenue with a man who held so many cards close to his chest?

"Is this how you operate, Mr. Darnell? Playing both sides, baiting those desperate for truth?"

"Truth is just a perspective, my dear. Those who control the narrative dictate the reality of it all. You'd do well to remember that." His gaze deepened, and a flicker of something darker crossed his features.

Elena took a moment, weighing her options. In this world of shadows, every choice could reverberate through the lives of those caught in its proximity.

"Are you familiar with someone named Julian Tavish?" she said, dropping the name into the conversation like a stone into still water. She saw his expression harden almost instantaneously.

"Whispers travel fast in this city," he replied, his tone chillingly even.

"I need to know if his name came up in relation to Francesca."

Darnell laughed softly, though the edge was unmistakable. "It's not what you think. Julian is an artist, not a political player. But then again, artists can have their own kind of darkness."

An unexpected interest flickered within her, a mixture of combativeness and intrigue. He knew more than he let on about connections between his world and hers.

"So you admit there's a connection then?"

"Ms. Rourke," he sighed, standing as he performed a dramatic flourish. "Your determination serves you well, but it blinds you to the reality that each thread you tug could lead to your unraveling."

"Is that a threat?" she shot back, brow raised.

"It's a warning, Elena," he clarified, moving towards the door. "If you're intent on solving this mystery, consider who truly holds the power in these negotiations. There are whispers of deals far more treacherous than the truth of Francesca's disappearance."

His voice lowered once more, infectious with tenacity.

"With each step, remember; loyalty is a delicate dance, one careless misstep may plunge you into the abyss. You heard the stories; it's about who you trust and when."

In that moment, Elena felt the full weight of his words, how they coiled around her like smoke and mirrors. Power, manipulation, and the corrosive nature of trust merged into one turbulent experience, knowing not just what to ask but also where each question might lead her.

Stepping from the golden cage of Darnell's office was like emerging from a chrysalis, the scalding glare of reality waiting just outside those well-guarded doors. She understood now that each player in this precarious game operated under their own set of rules, and she was tumbling headfirst into a world where all was scrutiny divided by an invisible veil.

Elena left his office with far more than she had hoped to uncover. Darnell was a player, one of many she would have to navigate carefully, protecting her own secrets while unearthing those that others might not want exposed.

The lingering tension wrapped around her like a shroud, and a whispered caution echoed in her mind: as she ventured deeper into this web of complications, she must either learn to dance in the shadows or risk becoming ensnared within the darkness.

Outside, the city stretched before her, its pulse steady and hypnotic. She had come seeking truth, but now she understood it was shrouded in layers—layers defined by shadows, betrayals, and the complex fabric of human relationships.

The game was afoot, she reminded herself. And she was ready to play. Wherever it might lead.

Veiled Threats

Elena Rourke stepped into the lavish office of Senator Malcolm Voss, the air thick with the aroma of cigar smoke and the subtle undertone of expensive cologne. Dark wood paneling lined the room, adorned with photos of Voss shaking hands with dignitaries, their smiles mirroring the false charm that emanated from him. The senator himself sat behind a desk cluttered with papers, his sharp blue eyes glinting like cold steel under the golden glow of the overhead lamp.

"Elena, my dear," he crooned, leaning back in his leather chair, folding his hands over his belly. "I have heard so much about you. A rising star in our city. Would you like a drink?"

Elena forced herself to smile, masking the unease that churned within her. "No, thank you, Senator. I'm here about the socialite's disappearance—Margot LaRue. I believe you had some interactions with her before she went missing."

Voss raised an eyebrow, a flicker of something dangerous passing across his features. "Oh, Margot. A lovely creature, indeed. The press has a knack for turning a simple disappearance into a spectacle, don't you think?" He chuckled, but the sound came out hollow.

Elena crossed her arms, steadying her thoughts. "Simplicity or spectacle aside, she is still a person, Senator. I need to know what you discussed during your meetings."

"Discussions of a political nature, naturally. Nothing scandalous, I assure you. Just pleasant conversations over dinner parties. Margot had a way of lighting up the room, captivating with her stories. But politics can be a dangerous game, dear. One must tread lightly."

Suddenly, the tone shifted. Voss leaned forward, his gaze piercing into hers. "And you, Elena, would do well to remember that some questions are better left unasked. Secrets can be terribly burdensome, and should they find the wrong ears, may even come with consequences."

The weight of his words hung between them like a tightrope, each phrase laced with a veiled threat.
Elena's pulse quickened as she met his intimidating stare. "I'm aware of the risks, Senator. That's why I'm here. To uncover the truth."

He chuckled softly, tapping his fingers against the desk, a calculated nonchalance in his posture. "Ah, the truth. Such a slippery concept. You see, my dear, in my line of work, not everything is as it seems. Every question leads to another, and the more layers you peel back, the more chaotic the world becomes."

With every word, Voss reminded her just how entangled she was in a game much larger than herself.
The senator's demeanor oscillated between charm and menace, every syllable a carefully crafted dagger aimed at her resolve.
"What are you insinuating?" Elena's voice was steady, fueled by determination despite the anxiety simmering beneath her calm surface.

Voss smiled, revealing a row of perfectly aligned teeth. "Insinuating? Oh dear, that would imply I am assuming too much. I prefer to operate with facts. It's the uncertainty of your inquiries that concerns me, Elena. Ignorance can be bliss, but knowledge can lead to peril. I wouldn't want you to run afoul of the wrong people."

She leaned forward, lips forming a line without betraying the flicker of doubt. "Is that a threatening warning, Senator?"

With a dramatic flourish, he picked up a glass of whiskey, swirling the amber liquid as if considering the weight of her question. "I find it fascinating how brave professionals become when they perceive themselves as untouchable. But make no mistake—the web stretches far and wide in this city. You would do well to keep your inquiries in check."

Elena's heart raced as tension crackled in the air. Every word he wove seemed to wrap around her like chains—tightening an already heavy feeling in the pit of her stomach.
"I am not afraid of navigating dark waters, Senator. This investigation could shed light where there has been nothing but shadows."

His laughter rolled through the room, cold and mocking. "Oh, such conviction. But you must ask yourself, at what cost? Innocent souls can get caught in the crossfire, and when lives are at stake, one must reconsider their role in the narrative."

It was becoming painfully clear that Voss was entangled in the city's intricate web of deceit, his charm masking layers of ulterior motives.
Elena straightened her posture, defiance and determination battling with the sense of danger that loomed in the room.

"If you have something to hide, I suggest you reconsider your next moves. I will find out what happened to Margot, and it won't matter who stands in my way."

He placed the glass down with a deliberate clink, and for a moment, an edge of sadness graced his features. "You are indeed spirited, Elena. It's a noble trait. But you see, curiosity can be a hazardous affair. I can't guarantee your safety should you choose to dig too deep."

"Or perhaps you can guarantee it if I keep my investigations shallow and my questions unasked," she shot back, conviction wrapping tightly around her like armor.

Voss's demeanor shifted, the ghost of a storm brewing behind his self-assured façade. "You think you have the strength to challenge a man like me? I have power, connections, and the capacity to make your life quite difficult should you persist in this charade. It would be a shame if your ambition led to your undoing."

The implications of his words coiled around her thoughts, chilling her resolve, but nothing could extinguish the fire ignited in her spirit.

"Is that a threat or a plea for self-preservation, Senator?" Elena provoked, testing the waters of his impending fury.

For a moment, his expression hardened, the charming mask slipping. "Do not confuse my candor with weakness, Elena. The wheels of power are in motion, and they do not hesitate to crush those who become inconveniences. And trust me; I have no qualms about being ruthless when it comes to protecting my interests."

"Your interests, or your truths?"

She held his gaze, steadying herself against the palpable intensity. Fear trembled in her chest, but she pushed it aside.

Voss studied her carefully, like a predator weighing its prey. He leaned forward, the atmosphere thickening with threat.

"Be careful, dear. Sometimes, the truth is a heavy burden. You might find your sanity unraveling. And I won't lose sleep should you choose to ignore my warnings."

Elena's heart beat against her ribs like a war drum. "You think intimidation will make me back down? I've faced worse than you, Voss."

He cocked his head, a glimmer of respect shimmering in his icy blue gaze, a short-lived moment of camaraderie amidst their escalating clash. "You have spirit, and that's commendable. But I'd hate to see you break that spirit in pursuit of your hollow ambitions. The truth is a dangerous game, and losing can cost you everything."

There it was again—the delicate dance between danger and allure, his words wrapping around her with steely precision.

"Is this your way of manipulating me? Trying to make me question my path?"

A dry smile tugged at the corners of Voss's mouth. "Manipulation is a tool for survival in my world, as it is in yours. But consider this: once you delve into the shadows, you run the risk of becoming one with the darkness."

The door swung open, breaking the tension for a brief second as Voss's assistant slid in, handing the senator a file. The shift in focus provided Elena with a fleeting moment of clarity as she observed the dynamic whirling around her.

If power influenced the senator so profoundly, she was determined not to falter in the face of that dark allure.

Voss took the file, his expression smoothing out again. "I'm afraid this discussion must end. My time is limited, but I trust you understand the implications of probing into affairs that may lead to unexpected revelations."

Elena stood, feeling the weight of his gaze following her movements, every lingering whisper thickening the tension in the air like fog rolling in off the ocean.

"Remember what I said," Voss cautioned, his voice low and heavy with unspoken power. "Following the shadows could lead you to places even you won't escape from. The walls have ears."

As she stepped back into the corridor, the chill of his veiled threat settled around her shoulders, wrapping her tightly as her pulse raced with a mix of exhilaration and fear.

The hallways were bustling with life, reality crashing back in with every thump of her heart—a stark contrast to the warped reality Voss had woven within his office.

In this tangled world, where motives shifted with the tide, she would not falter. No matter how high the stakes rose, she could not retract from the path laid out before her.

Elena's resolve only strengthened. The twisted underbelly of this city, steeped in secrets and betrayal, pulsed beneath her skin. Each step forward echoed a promise to unravel Voss's threats and lay bare the shadows that lurked in the corridors of power.

Yet now, with the predator aware of her every move, she questioned whether the risks she undertook could lead to not just the truth of Margot LaRue's disappearance, but also her own survival in a world where every smile concealed a hidden dagger.

The taste of danger was unsettling, invigorating; each question that remained unanswered propelled her further into the depths of her investigation and deeper into the shadows that accompanied her descent into darkness.

One way or another, the battle for the truth had begun. "Trust is a fickle companion, Elena," she murmured to herself as she stepped onto the neon-lit streets, resolved to face the treachery that lay ahead.

Connections Are Dangerous

Elena stepped away from the polished desk, the remnants of her conversation still buzzing in her ears. The glint of the city skyline filtered through the office window, casting long shadows across the room, and for a moment, it felt like the illusions created under that neon gaze were peeling away. Outside, sirens wailed, a haunting pulse that resonated with the unease churning deep within her. She wandered towards the glass, her reflection a mere ghost against the sprawling metropolis.

Trust is a fragile thread, she thought. The kind of thread that can snap at the slightest provocation, sending everything tumbling in ways most cannot imagine. This was not new to her. Elena had often navigated a world where loyalty was as disposable as the fleeting encounters punctuating her day, but the gravity of her current investigation rendered this truth sharper, more menacing.

Each interaction she had layered upon the last—hidden truths entwined with deceit. In her encounters with the femme fatale, the politician, and the artist, she had woven a delicate tapestry of intrigue and danger, each connection holding the potential for profound betrayal or unexpected alliance. Yet, she couldn't shake the feeling that beneath every charming smile and articulate promise lay the potential for treachery.

It was the artist's studio that haunted her thoughts most acutely. The stark contrast between his beautiful works of art and the chaos of his past mirrored her own internal turmoil. He had painted vivid landscapes from his pain, causing her to reflect on how her own trust—once a sturdy wall—had become a fragile façade hidden behind layers of emotional paint. Their shared vulnerability had felt like a breath of fresh air, yet it could also have masked dangerous undercurrents. What did he truly want from her? And in this dance of secrets, who was really leading?

She turned her gaze from the window, pacing the room as the shadows lengthened with the setting sun. Her mind raced with echoes of the encounters she had experienced recently. The political meeting—so cloaked in charm and deceit—where every word exchanged had the weight of veiled threats. The politician, with his slicked-back hair and silver tongue, had left her feeling unmoored, his intentions opaque even as he brandished his power. It was an encounter fraught with danger, one that had inadvertently tied her tighter to the city's corrupt heart.

Elena pictured his face, the way he had leaned in with that mock sincerity, promising help while subtly coercing her toward a course she had not intended. Connections like that could transform from sheer utility into nooses if she wasn't careful.

She had seen too many people drown in complexities that had started off innocently enough, yet morphed into entrapment.

And then there was the femme fatale—her allure an intoxicating mix of danger and seduction. The hotel lounge still played back in her mind like an aching song, the soft jazz interwoven with the tension that simmered just beneath the surface. Elena had never considered herself a woman easily drawn to temptation, yet the femme fatale had a way of weaving stories that made her hesitate, drawing her into a world that felt both glamorous and perilous. Every sultry glance was a thread pulling her deeper, but which way that path led remained to be seen. Was their connection a boon or a bane?

Elena found herself in a realm filled with reflections; every choice she had made so far felt like a ripple in the dark waters of deception. As she further examined the intertwining of her path with those around her, she could not ignore the tremors coursing through her resolve. How many times had she relied on others only to be left marred by disappointment or betrayal? The scars from those experiences ran deeper than any current wound.

It was late before she finally lowered herself into her chair, the weight of the day pressing heavily against her shoulders. With a deep, resolute breath, she set about organizing her thoughts. The files scattered across her desk were more than just papers filled with leads and tangents; they were embodiments of trust and deception, loyalty and betrayal. Each name had unfurled a different type of connection, and the threads of them all were starting to form a coherent pattern—or at least that was what she hoped.

She fiddled with a pen, rolling it between her fingers as she considered her next steps.

The missing socialite lingered in the peripheries, a haunting figure whose life unraveled into the very fabric of the society Elena was now entrenched in. How could Elena trust the narratives woven around her? Was she merely a pawn in a larger game? The stakes were raising with every passing hour.

Feeling overwhelmed, she picked up a photograph, one taken from the gala she had infiltrated. The socialite laughing amidst a cluster of high society elites seemed almost perfectly staged, yet the fleeting shadows crossing her face hinted at secrets untold. It was as if the photograph itself whispered allegations, beckoning an investigation into its glamour-soaked surface.

Elena's instincts kicked in as she laid the photo down; she needed allies who could help her get to the truth, yet that very act seemed laced with risk. She was becoming ensnared in a web of her own making. "Connections," she whispered to herself, mentally replaying the faces of those close to her—since the beginning of this case, she had entangled herself with people she did not fully understand.

The journey had twisted her moral compass, compelling her to sidestep her own values. The femme fatale, the politician, even the artist—each had become players on a chessboard, and Elena was at the center, unaware of the ultimate checkmate that loomed just out of view.

With every twist and turn in the case, an intricate dance unfolded—alliances formed, and slowly but surely, trust began to erode. It shattered every time she questioned another's motives. Pieces of herself became consumed in this landscape littered with betrayal; the question that burned in her mind was whether she could emerge unscathed.

Shaking off the creeping dread, she pulled out a notebook filled with observations and connections, a tapestry burgeoning with the names and motives of those she had met. It was a board saturated with colliding lives and intersecting destinies—all ultimately tied to her central case: the socialite.

Flipping through the pages, she saw the evidence of her encounters laid bare before her. She recalled the different individuals and their respective shadows—each person represented a choice, a danger swirling under the surface, their motivations obscured by the masks they wore. And slowly, it became clear that connections were not merely routes to finding the truth; they were potential traps, each circle closing tighter around her, escalating the threat of the world she had chosen to step into.

The thought made her heart race, each beat a reminder of the risks she sprinted toward with all haste.

As the shadows deepened in her office, she leaned back in her chair, the faint creak echoing in the silence. She was on the brink of something monumental—an investigation that could either fortify her position or shatter her completely. But within this turbulent uncertainty, she felt unchanged, true to her core. Despite the chaos of her connections, she held fast to her own truth.

Yet she knew enough to be cautious; this was not a game where emotions served well, nor a landscape where compassion would safeguard her. No, the connections she cultivated now would require discernment and calculated risks. She could not afford to allow her emotions to cloud her judgment when navigating this newfound territory.

The web she had spun was intricate, interconnected by invisible strands of trust and ambition, loyalty and distrust. And like that, she resolved to untangle these threads with diligence. She must analyze each connection, scrutinizing not only the individuals but the motivations behind their actions. Something inside her lit with resolve. Amidst the turmoil, she would carve clarity from chaos.

As she reviewed her notes, a familiar name caught her eye—the artist. He had been more than a mere fortuitous ally; he reeked of contradictions, captivating yet alarming, providing glimpses into the depth of the socialite's past.

Elena had felt a connection with him that clouded her judgment. Their emotional exchanges, juxtaposed with the seductive allure of his artistry, created an intoxicating blend of danger and intimacy—one that could easily blind her to the realities of their associations.

Fueled by newfound determination, she picked up the pen and began to chart his connections, mapping out the potential shadows that surrounded him. She needed to uncover whether he was a mere reflection of her own struggles or if he was entangled in the same web that held the missing socialite—a mosaic of suffering and deception that could lead her to ruin.

With each doodle and note, Elena knew she had to separate genuine allies from those who thrived on lies. A sense of urgency enveloped her as she realized that each 'beyond the surface' conversation she had ever engaged in could potentially lead to pivotal moments illuminating or obscuring her path.

But perhaps the most unsettling revelation of all was the truth residing within her.

The emotions she thought she could compartmentalize began to gnaw at her; could she truly be objective amid all these messy connections? It would be a test of her resolve—embracing her vulnerability while maintaining a shield against the deceptions that lay beneath.

The sun dipped lower, casting rays through her window almost like a spotlight on her increasing sense of urgency. Each moment her investigation lingered without resolution heightened the stakes—she could no longer proceed with hopeful optimism. The choices ahead seemed more daunting than mere investigations; they would demand a reckoning with the very foundations of her principles.

As night fell, she savored the last light of day, knowing she would need grit to navigate this web with deft precision. The shadows spilled deeper into her office, aligning with her own fears of the unknown. But she was not one to shy away from danger. It had always been the weight of choices that buried her in uncertainty—not the act of stepping forward. And now, as those choices began aligning into a clearer picture, she felt compelled to forge ahead.

Elena cast one last look at the reflection in the window, a woman at the intersection of light and shadow. The ephemeral connections she fostered would either lead her to the truth or entrap her in a cycle of deception. Either way, she was resolved. With a deep breath, she pushed her chair back and stepped away from her desk, determination anchoring her steps as if they were laden with purpose, guiding her towards an unknown future steeped in uncertainty.

Underneath it all, a whisper of hope bloomed—a dim but persistent light amidst encroaching darkness as she prepared to step once more into a world of danger, navigating the jagged labyrinth of fate with eyes wide open.

Twisted Loyalties

The Weight of Betrayal

Elena Rourke stood in the dim light of her cramped office, the weight of betrayal heavy in her chest. The walls, adorned with peeling wallpaper and the faint scent of dust, bore witness to countless cases that passed through her hands over the years. Each file, a testimony to the secrets she had unearthed, each photograph—a frozen glimpse into the lives of those who sought her help. But today, it felt different. Today, it felt personal.

With the clock ticking mercilessly on the wall, Elena flipped through the latest report, her fingers trembling as she traced the inked details of a crime she had initially believed was solvable—a missing socialite named Victoria Lux. Her case had started as a tantalizing puzzle, each clue like a thread in a tapestry she was determined to untangle. But as the days morphed into sleepless nights and faces of familiar mentors transformed into shadows of doubt, she realized that the investigation was spiraling into an abyss she hadn't foreseen.

Just yesterday, she had received a tip from Ben, a friend from her college years and a colleague who worked in local law enforcement.

He had assured her of his support, boasting about having her back as she ventured deeper into the domain of the city's glittering elite. His smile had been disarming, reassuring. Yet tonight, that smile felt like a mask hiding something sinister.

Elena's mind drifted back to a warm evening spent in a rickety bar, laughter echoing as friends gathered to celebrate her small victories. She could still hear the echoes of joy wrapped in the clink of glasses, feel the warmth of camaraderie enveloping them like a well-worn blanket. It was a reprieve from the darkness that often shadowed them. Yet, intertwined with those joyous flashes was the faint chill of doubt—faces flickering with moments of discomfort she hadn't understood at the time.

Ben's laughter had rolled like thunder through the smoky air, and in that moment, she had wanted to believe in him. To believe that her friends were allies against the undercurrents of the city's corruption. But as she leaned back in her chair, the whispered reminders that Ben had a foot in each world crawled back to the fore. The night they shared the stage with bottled spirits, he spoke of police work with both pride and frustration; discontent was never far from his lips. Was it possible that he had straddled the line of morality too closely?

The phone on her desk rang, pulling her from the nostalgia. The shrill sound cut through the silence, startling her. Taking a deep breath, she answered, knowing that each ring held the potential for news, for new threads to unravel.

"Elena, it's me." The voice on the other end was shaky.

"Ben?"

"I need to meet. Can we talk?" His tone betrayed a sense of urgency she had not heard before, twisting like a knife in her side. Uncertainty twisted her stomach.

"Sure. Where?"

"Meet me at Clara's Diner in thirty. I'll explain everything." Click.

The line went dead, leaving the hollow echo of his voice resonating in her ears. She had always respected Ben for his ability to cut through the noise of the city's lies, but now she couldn't shake the feeling of dread encompassing her.

Elena stood up, smoothed her blazer, and strode out of her office. The streets outside felt claustrophobic, tightly packed with whispers and secrets that magnified her anxiety. Each step was heavy, a reminder of the rift growing between her and everything she had trusted. The city's neon lights struggled against the encroaching darkness, flickering like faint whispers—warnings or curses, she couldn't yet discern.

As she approached Clara's Diner, the familiar sign glowed invitingly, but an inexplicable chill seeped into her skin. There was something about the atmosphere tonight that didn't feel right. The clatter of dishes and hum of conversations blurred into background noise as she entered. She spotted Ben in a booth toward the far end, his fingers nervously tapping against the plastic surface.

"Hey." She slid into the booth across from him, taking in his pale complexion—a stark contrast to his usual robust demeanor.

"Thanks for coming," he murmured, glancing around, as if afraid of being overheard.

"What's going on?" Elena prompted, the tension creeping into her voice.

"I have to tell you something important, something about your case," he said, swallowing hard. His eyes darted around again, weighing the words that hung heavy in the air. It felt as if the gravity of the moment was pulling them closer together, yet creating an unbridgeable chasm of mistrust.

"Just tell me, Ben," she urged, leaning in.

He hesitated, before finally speaking, "Victoria Lux…she—" his words faltered. "She wasn't just a socialite. She was involved in something bigger than I thought." He paused, the silence between them thickening as the weight of what he was about to share loomed over them. "I know you've been digging into her life, but you need to understand—I think there's more to her disappearance."

Elena felt her heart rate quicken, adrenaline surging through her veins. "What do you mean?"

"I wasn't sure how to tell you. The department has been under pressure from some powerful people. There's talk…rumors of corrupt ties to her family and dealings that stretch beyond anything I imagined. I didn't want you to get caught in the crossfire," he explained, his voice barely above a whisper.

Betrayal cut deep. The words clawed at her thoughts, intertwining with memories she had fought to grasp. Was Ben warning her, or was he merely trying to deflect his own involvement?

"What do you mean? You've known that I've been involved in this investigation. How could you keep this from me?" she shot back, biting her tongue to suppress the rising tide of anger.

"I didn't know until recently," he insisted, his alibi shaky. "I've had my ear to the ground. You have to understand, some files…they're gone. Someone's cleaning up, and I can't let you walk into that alone." The weight of betrayal on his face mirrored the depths of her disappointment, twisting her gut even more.

Elena felt her resolve falter as she looked into Ben's eyes. The warmth of their friendship had provided refuge in past storms, yet now, the fire that had once flickered seemed extinguished. The foundation of their alliance felt fractured, hints of a double-cross simmering beneath the surface.

"I thought you were on my side, Ben. Helping me piece together Victoria's life. Now it feels like I'm standing alone in a void," she replied bitterly, punctuating her disappointment.

He opened his mouth, but words failed him. All the arguments he might have raised felt feeble against the rising tide of suspicion.

"Do you even realize the implications of this?" she continued, her emotions spiraling. "If people are hiding information, it means they're conniving in ways I haven't even begun to comprehend. Why should I trust you now?"

"It's complicated!" he hissed, leaning across the table, desperation painted across his features. "I'm trying to protect you!"

"But protect me from what? Your secrets? The more you hide, the more I wonder if you're folded into this mess. I'm thrusting myself into the depths; I need everyone to be honest!"

Silence enveloped them, thickening with unsaid words dangling in the air. Elena remained resolute, fighting the tide of memories that twisted her perception of their shared past.

"In this city, there are no allies, only those waiting for the right moment to betray," she said coldly, each word dropping between them like stones in a well.

Ben recoiled at her sentiment, a flicker of rage sparking in his eyes. "I've never betrayed you. I'd never…"

Elena interrupted, not willing to forgive, "But how can I know that now? Loyalty wears thin in a place like this. I thought we were fighting together, and here you are, veiling everything behind shadowy truths."

Even now, in her heart, she longed for the tie that bonded them for years. Through thick and thin, they had sidestepped the chaos of life together, unearthing secrets, sharing small triumphs over late-night shifts.

Yet now, their laughter echoed like taunts against the stark reality of clandestine forces at play; a betrayal lurking silently in the depths of their city's most glamorous facades. Her memories twisted into shadows, taunting her optimism with stark reminders of his ambivalence.

Ben leaned back, frustration crinkled across his forehead. "What do you want from me, Elena? I'm risking my job just to warn you."

"I want honesty. I want you to give me the truth that's hidden behind all these layers!" she exclaimed, louder than intended, drawing the gaze of nearby patrons.

"The truth is ugly!" he spat, gripping the table as if holding on would quell the growing rift between them. "Victoria is wrapped up in things you have no idea about. There's fear woven into this chaos. Powerful people involved—"

With measured calm, Elena cut him off, "Don't you think I've gathered that by now? But I cannot stand idly by while both you and the system you represent are puppeteering me into something more sinister!"

Ben's jaw clenched tight; for a moment, they merely stared at each other, gauging the distance that had grown between them.

Elena didn't care to decipher the frail strings of friendship; the betrayal she felt left marks deeper than words. She rose abruptly, leaving the uneven tiles of the diner behind her as she walked out, feeling the fragility of their connection shatter.

The night air was a stark contrast to the warmth inside the diner, filled with the adrenaline of veiled emotions along with the bitter chill draft she couldn't shake. As she stepped into the street, her mind echoed back to all the times she had defended Ben—yet, here they stood, a chasm separating them as if years had passed unnoticed.

Elena's phone buzzed, pulling her away from her spiraling thoughts. A new message flashed on the screen, a clue that had escaped her before. As she read, the implications twisted her own narrative further still. The names mentioned in Ben's warning—those who danced around power—were suddenly emerging clearer, like specters in the darker corners of the investigation.

In the moments to come, she realized that all along, betrayal wormed its way through every layer she thought she had trusted.

Ben's face flickered in her mind, his pleas now colored with a different intent as she transformed through this nightmare, the city breathing heavy around her while every shadow grew darker.

The stark truth cut deep as she walked past the familiar confines of the city—this wasn't just about Victoria anymore. It was personal. She had to go deeper, to pierce through the cloud of betrayal enveloping her. Each step felt charged with purpose, like a razor edge against the reality that threatened to consume everything she held dear. How could she navigate this labyrinth when the very people she relied upon concealed their own agendas?

This line of questioning would lead her back into the fray, to confront the silent whispers of loyalty tangled with strings of deceit. The path before her was dangerous, yet the tumult of betrayal ignited a new determination—her investigation was only beginning, and she had to discover where each link led in this treacherous game.

Elena swore to unravel every secret with fire in her heart. The city bustled with life, oblivious to the storm brewing within her. With each piece of the puzzle, she harnessed the chaos swirling inside and forged a new alliance, one born from the shards of broken trust, even if it pushed her closer to darkness.

A Decision of Allies

Elena stood at the edge of the chaos, the rising tension wrapping around her like a shroud. The city outside her modest office window was alive with noise—sirens wailing, voices shouting, a constant hum of agitation that created a symphony of dread. Inside, however, silence reigned, thick with unspoken words and heavy with unshed tears. Time warped around her, each second pulsating with uncertainty as she wrestled with the decisions that lay in front of her.

The flashing neon lights from the streets below illuminated the dim room, casting flickering shadows on the walls, mirroring the turmoil roiling within her. She paced, her instincts urging her to make a decision, to confront the shadows that had crept too close to her heart. The remnants of her investigation weighed on her—a tangled web of betrayals and alliances that threatened to suffocate her if she didn't act soon.

Her mind drifted to Alex, her longtime confidant and friend, the one person she had relied upon as the walls of her life crumbled around her. Their connection had always been a silent promise, a bond that had seen them through the storms of their pasts. But in recent days, doubt had begun to gnaw at her, sowing seeds of mistrust where once there had been only loyalty. Their alliance, once a source of strength, now felt like a fragile house of cards, teetering dangerously close to collapse.

Elena's heart raced as she contemplated the confrontation looming ahead. A quick glance at the clock on her desk revealed the time was slipping away faster than she could manage. She reached for her phone, hesitating for a moment before dialing Alex's number. The familiar ring echoed in the silence, a haunting reminder of how easily trust could be shattered.

"Hey," Alex's voice came through the line, steady yet tinged with the gravity of their situation.

"Can we meet?" Elena asked, her voice steadier than she felt.

A beat of silence fell between them before Alex replied, "You sound serious. Is everything okay?"

"Far from it. Can we just meet? Please?"

"Sure. Where?"

"Dead Drop at eight."

A pause lingered before he replied, "I'll be there."

After ending the call, Elena slumped into her chair, her heart pounding in her chest. The Dead Drop was a bar on the outskirts of the city; it was dimly lit and concealed behind layers of grime and neglect—a fitting place for their discussion. She knew that secrets thrived within its walls, and tonight, she needed to ensure that hers didn't suffocate under the weight of uncertainty.

As the hours stretched on, she prepared herself for the inevitable confrontation. Elena gathered her thoughts while trying to compartmentalize the emotions swirling in her mind. Memories flooded back: their shared laughter, the quiet moments of understanding when no words were needed, the feeling of safety when Alex was nearby. But with those memories also came the specters of friendship—skeletons in the closet that she could no longer ignore.

When the clock struck eight, she found herself standing at the bar, the air thick with the scent of whiskey and desperation. The low lighting wrapped around her, cocooning her in anonymity as she awaited Alex's arrival. Her breath quickened as the door swung open; the familiar figure stepped inside, his expression serious and guarded. She waved him over, the slight motion carrying all the weight of her unresolved doubts and fears.

"Hey," Alex greeted, sliding onto the barstool next to her. His eyes searched her face, reading every flicker of anxiety she could not conceal.

"What's going on, Elena? You seemed off on the phone," he prodded, his voice low and laced with concern.

"I… I don't know where to start." She felt the lump rising in her throat.

"We can start with what's bothering you," he suggested, leaning closer. "You're not in trouble, are you?"

The question hung in the air, a fragile thread of concern between them. Elena hesitated, then forged ahead. "It's about the case—the missing socialite. I've stumbled onto something… something big. But I can't shake this feeling that I'm in over my head."

"Over your head? You've always handled tough cases, Elena. What's different this time?" His brows furrowed as he leaned back, arms crossed, a defensive shield against the impending tempest.

"Everything feels… skewed," she admitted, her voice cracking under the weight of her confession.

"I've been digging through layers of lies, and there are connections I never anticipated. I thought we were in this together. But now, I'm not so sure."

Alex's silence was deafening, a crack in the alliance she had relied upon. "What do you mean?" he asked, careful and measured.

"I mean—" she took a deep breath, searching for words that felt slippery against her tongue, "I mean, what if you know more than you're telling me? What if you've got secrets that put me at risk?"

The accusation hung between them, vibrating with tension. Unexpectedly, Alex laughed, a short, bitter sound that felt like nails on chalkboard. "Elena, how long have we known each other?" he asked.

"Long enough. Too long to discount this feeling," she countered, meeting his gaze head-on. "You can't deny that something feels off. Not with everything happening around us."

He leaned in, lowering his voice. "Do you really think I would betray you? After everything?"

Elena's heart sank at his words; they were laced with defensiveness and conflict. "I don't know what to think anymore, Alex. Every time I uncover a thread, it leads me to another circle of lies. People I've trusted have been deceiving me, and I'm scared."

"Scared of what?"

"Scared to believe in the alliances I've built. Scared that I might have put my trust in the wrong people." The admission fell from her lips like ash, bitter and heavy.

"And what about me? All these years, I've been the first one you called. You once said we shared a connection that couldn't be broken. Does that mean nothing to you now?" His voice softened, but he didn't back down.

"It means everything, Alex. But I need to know where you really stand. This isn't just about trust; it's about survival." Her words were raw, fueled by urgency and fear.

"Let's assume for a moment that I know more than I've said," he pressed on. "What would you do?"

"Confront you," she replied, her pulse racing. "That's why we're here."

A sudden silence enveloped them, palpable and charged. The weight of her words hung in the space between them, heavy with a certainty that neither could evade. Alex's brows furrowed deeper as he contemplated her, the tension stretching like a tightrope straining beneath their weight.

"You think you can just waltz in here and throw accusations around?" he finally said, his voice low and simmering with uncharacteristic anger.

"I'm not throwing accusations. I'm being honest, and I'm terrified of what I might uncover."

"But you're asking me to bear the brunt of your fear. Do you realize that?" he shot back, frustration spilling from his tone.

"I realize that our alliance is built on the foundation of trust!" Elena countered, her own emotions threatening to spill over.

"And what do you do when that trust is called into question? You start doubting the connections that helped you stay afloat? Is that what this is?"

"Yes!" The word slipped out before she could contain it. "It is! I can't afford to be around someone who might be a liar, Alex. I can't die because I refused to ask the hard questions." As the words poured out, she could hear the tremor in her voice.

His expression softened, allowing a measure of their shared history to seep back in. "Elena, what happened to the woman who fought through the darkness, who never backed down from any threat?"

"The same woman who is terrified of losing the one person she cares about most," she replied, her voice dipping into vulnerability.

"Here's the truth, then," he exhaled sharply, running a hand through his hair. "I'm at risk too. We are both playing a game where trust is an enemy just as much as silence."

"What does that mean for us?" she whispered.

"It means you need to be cautious, but it also means I'm right here—ready to fight for our truth. I'm not your enemy, but I can't have you questioning our bond without reason." He leaned closer, his intensity locking her in place. "Let's clear the air. No more doubt, no more shadows between us. Let's face whatever's lurking in the dark."

"Can you promise me that?" she breathed, her heart racing as loyalty battled with suspicion.

"I can," he replied, resolve igniting in his voice. "But can you promise me that you will trust me enough to share your fears? We don't stand a chance split apart."

Their eyes locked, an unspoken pact forming amid the swirling undercurrents of their conversation. The previous warmth of their friendship mingled with tension, a complexity that transformed their fragile alliance into something deeper—a willingness to risk everything for each other. In that moment, she felt the remnants of doubt begin to fragment, replaced with something far more potent: a desire to protect what they had built together.

"Okay," she finally said, the word escaping her lips like a soft sigh. "I'll trust you. But you have to be honest with me—no secrets."

"Noted," Alex said, his voice finally filled with relief as they held each other's gaze.

But with their alliance reaffirmed, the weight of their predicament loomed larger than before.

"Together, then?" Elena asked, her voice barely above a whisper as she peered into his eyes, searching for reassurance.

"Together," he affirmed, taking her hand in his.

Yet even as their fingers interlocked, the looming shadows swallowed their moment whole. Both were acutely aware that trust was no longer a guarantee. It had morphed into an unpredictable beast that could easily unravel the fragile threads of their alliance.

Elena's heart swelled with a mixture of hope and apprehension as they stepped back into the storm of deception and betrayal. The city beyond the bar pulsed with life, unaware of the secrets that twisted through the veins of its streets. They were allies bound by fate and fear, confronting the darkness together, aware that time would reveal if their loyalty would be tested once again.

In the bar's dim light, Elena and Alex reemerged as a united front, ready to navigate the treacherous waters of an increasingly chaotic world, their futures intertwined like fragile threads in the hands of fate. But deep down, the echo of uncertainty lingered. The question of what loyalty meant in a place where alliances could shift like quicksand loomed ominously, and as they walked out into the neon-lit night, she knew in her heart that this was only the calm before the storm.

Bound by Secrets

Elena stood in the dim glow of her office, the shadows of the city sprawling beyond the window. The once comforting haze of night now felt oppressive, a weight pressing down on her chest as memories of the past few days coursed through her mind. Shattered loyalties were pieces of glass scattered across her psyche, each sharp fragment reflecting a truth she feared to confront.

The air was heavy with anticipation, tension looming like storm clouds on the horizon. She leaned against the older mahogany desk that had seen better days, the surface cluttered with cases she once found intriguing but now lay forgotten. The missing socialite's case had shifted from a simple inquiry into a labyrinth of intrigue, and the more she unraveled, the more she felt ensnared.

The light of her desk lamp flickered, casting erratic shadows in the room. Outside, the streets were drenched in the faint afterglow of neon signs, pulses of the city's heartbeat that felt ominously disconnected from her own. A siren echoed in the distance, a chilling reminder of the chaos just outside her door.

The call from Theo, her trusted informant, still rang in her ears. It had been hurried, frantic—a whispered warning laced with urgency. "Elena, there's more to the socialite's story than anyone knows. You're not safe," he had said, his voice barely above a whisper as if the shadows of the city could overhear their conversation.

"More secrets?" she had replied, a mixture of skepticism and curiosity bubbling up inside her. Was there ever a shortage of secrets in this city? For every clue she chased, another truth lay waiting, shrouded in obscurity.

"Listen, I can't say much over the phone. Meet me at the alley behind The Velvet Room. Midnight." The line had gone dead before she could respond, leaving her with an unsettling sense of anticipation. The Velvet Room—a notorious haunt for the city's elite, where secrets were bartered like currency amid the clinking of glasses.

Elena's mind raced through plausible outcomes as she prepared for the meeting. She slipped into her coat, the long fabric brushing against her legs, and felt the reassuring weight of her service pistol nestled in her holster beneath her arm. It was an unwelcome companion but necessary in a world that thrived on betrayal.

When she arrived at the alley behind The Velvet Room, a chill danced along her spine. Dimly lit, the alleyway was lined with bricks stained by years of neglect and the residue of countless secrets whispered among shadows. It smelled faintly of rain and something more sinister, an olfactory warning of what lay ahead.

"Theo?" she called, her voice steady despite the tightening knot of anxiety in her stomach. Silence answered her, thick and heavy, pressing on her senses like a mallet.

Then, from the darkness, a figure emerged, his silhouette stark against the flickering streetlights. Theo stepped forward, his eyes darting around as if fearful of unseen watchers. He was dressed in a dark jacket that did little to hide the tension in his posture.

"It's bad, Elena," he said, his voice low, almost breathless. "Whatever you think you know—it's only the surface. The socialite isn't just missing; she's tangled in a web of power and deceit that threads through this entire city."

Theo's words were like a dark fog rolling in, threatening to envelop her in despair. She gestured for him to continue, and he looked away, the shadows flickering across his face like ghostly fingers.

"I've heard whispers about powerful people being involved…dangerous people." He paused for effect, drawing in a breath as if the revelation weighed heavily on him. "Her family isn't what they appear to be. There are debts, vendettas, even lies manufactured for the public eye."

"Who?" Elena pressed, driven by her relentless pursuit of the truth.

His lips pursed, struggling to form the words. "The politician, Collins. He's been linked to her family—more than just a friend. They all play a role in this twisted play. And it's not just him... there are two others. I can't tell you everything, but enough to keep your eyes wide open."

Elena crossed her arms, fighting to mask her unease. Collins was a man she had grown to distrust—his charm couldn't disguise the serpent lurking beneath his carefully crafted image. "You said two others. Who?"

Theo hesitated, glancing over his shoulder as if the shadows had ears. "A prominent social figure in the charity scene and… well, an artist. A painter who spent time with her. They were close." His expression faltered, a flicker of unease reflecting in his eyes.

"Elena, the truth goes deeper than what you see. There's a lot at stake here, and you might want to rethink how deep you want to dive into this."

Her mind raced like a train barreling down the tracks. An artist connected to the socialite? Memories flooded back—a brief encounter with a man who had painted sorrow with violent strokes, unearthing emotions better left buried.

"Who? What's his name?"

Theo's face darkened. "I don't know, but he's been involved in these circles for a while. You'll need to investigate—be careful." His eyes lingered on hers for a moment too long, a silent plea mingled with an urgent warning.

"I will," she promised, but beneath the conviction lay an unsettling sense of foreboding, as if she had stumbled into a minefield with no clear path ahead.

As the clock struck midnight, Elena felt the weight of revelation settle over her, raw and pulsating like an open wound. She nodded, exchanging silent goodbyes with Theo before parting ways, the shadows swallowing him whole once more.

The artist's name echoed in her mind as she navigated the tangled web. A painter bound by shadows, thorns intertwined with beauty. She felt the urge to seek him out, yet a twisted sense of caution in her gut pulled her back. Was he a key to understanding the blurring lines of loyalty, or yet another player hiding behind a mask?

She hurried back to her office, driving through quiet streets now bathed in artificial light—each shadow a reminder of the murky alliances that encroached on her life. Lines were drawn, and with every revelation, each person she grew closer to threatened to unravel the fragile trust she had invested in them.

Elena rifled through her papers, fragments of information sprawled across her desk. Photos of the missing socialite, scribbled notes, whispered conversations—all points in a constellation of mystery that now felt unbearably heavy. She needed clarity, a path that connected the scattered evidence across her mind, yet every answer brought forth new questions.

Without hesitation, she seized the photograph of the artist she barely remembered, his paint-splattered hands and sorrowful gaze locked in time like a frozen moment of vulnerability. His name escaped her, but his presence lingered like a haunting melody.

"I need answers," she muttered to herself.

The decision was almost compulsive. Without waiting, she made the call to an old acquaintance who frequented the underground art scene, a connection who could lead her to the tortured artist and uncover the web of their shared secrets. As she dialed, an uneasy feeling settled over her—one of those deep-seated instincts that begged her to tread lightly, to be wary of the betrayals that danced at the peripheries of her vision.

Hours later, she found herself in a dimly lit gallery, one that exuded an aura of desperation mingled with creativity—a haven for the broken and beautifully flawed. The muted clamor of conversations washed over her as she navigated through veils of bodies, eyes scanning the walls adorned with emotional chaos captured within strokes of color.

Among the crowd, she spotted a familiar face—Renée, the gossipy socialite who had a knack for snooping around the truth. With her hair styled to perfection and eyes iced with a hint of mischief, she didn't belong here; she was just as out of place as Elena.

"Elena! Darling, it's been too long!" Renée cooed, her voice dripping with saccharine charm. "What brings you to this little corner of darkness?"

Elena forced a smile, trying to mask her motives. "I'm looking for someone. Heard he might be here."

"Ooh! An artist? I can smell the drama already. Have you met the subject of the rumors?" Renée leaned closer, her eyes sparkling with intrigue.

"He's a tortured genius, you know—painted his way through heartache and desire. Such a shame about the missing woman, isn't it?"

"The more I peel away the layers, the more it's all connected," Elena replied coolly, focusing on the task at hand. "Do you know where I can find him?"

Renée twirled a strand of hair around her finger, clearly enjoying this little game. "You know, love, truths are slippery things—hard to grasp yet heavier than anticipated. But if you're looking for answers, I might know just the way."

Elena narrowed her eyes, sensing Renée's undercurrent of mischief, yet she bit back her instincts. Time was of the essence, and Renée could inadvertently lead her to valuable information.

"Fine, but no games, Renée. I don't have time for your theatrics."

With a dramatic huff, Renée motioned toward the far end of the gallery where an artist's easel towered in the flickering light. "You should make haste. But remember, darling, every stroke has its cost."

With a quick nod, Elena pushed through the crowd, her determination pulse quickening as she approached the easel. The artist stood in a world of his own, breath shallow and eyes lost within the canvas. It was here—this chaotic dance of colors and emotions reflected back like shadows bleeding into daylight.

"Excuse me," she said, interrupting his focused trance.

He turned, surprise flickering across his features, followed by a guarded bristle. "What do you want?"

"I need to talk."

"About what?" He regarded her with a mix of skepticism and curiosity, as if gauging her intentions from the tip of her shoes to the depths of her soul.

"It's about the socialite," she pressed, forcing her voice to remain steady despite the rising tide of emotions within.

A flicker of recognition flashed across his face, but he quickly concealed it with a mask of indifference. "I don't know anything about that."

"Bull," Elena spat, frustration surging. "You were part of her life—your names are tied together in whispers across the city. I need to know what you were to her."

His gaze sharpened, and she could see the way his guarded demeanor cracked ever so slightly. "What's it to you?" he countered, his voice an icy challenge.

"I'm trying to help. If you care about her at all, you'll want to talk," she replied, her heart thrumming in her chest.

"I didn't care for her the way you think," he said, eyes darting beyond her shoulder as if seeking an escape route. "She was just another part of a world I'm trying to leave."

"What do you want to leave behind?" Her voice dropped, a lure weaving through her words. "Let me help you."

The moment stretched into the silence that loomed between them, palpable and fraught with unsaid truths. He finally leaned forward, a mixture of resignation and rebellion etched into his features. "Fate binds us all, doesn't it? Secrets and shadows. She was not just a socialite; she was a thread woven into lives far darker than her own."

"Tell me," she urged, her desperation palpable now, a crack in the concrete despair that festered within them both.

The artist glanced around before leaning closer, whispering. "She found herself in a place too dangerous—a place where echoes of debts were never extinguished. People wanted to keep her hidden for different reasons—Collins, especially..."

The name hit her like a slap in the face. "Why?"

"The two of them had a connection—twisted, but something deeper than just political game-playing. Collins had plans. They always do when it comes to someone like her. She was a pawn, and the moment she started to fight back, she became collateral."

Instinct kicked in, the weight of truth colliding with her sense of purpose. "What do you mean? Fight back how?"

"Let's just say she wasn't the docile creature everyone believed her to be. She had a voice—one that could expose the lies that wrap this city in darkness. That made her dangerous."

As he spoke, Elena's thoughts spun into chaos, a whirlwind of connections leading toward uncharted territory.

"Why didn't you come forward sooner?"

"I was shackled by my own fears," he replied, voice strained. "But the night she disappeared, I was with her. She was scared, threatened."

"You—what?" The realization struck her with brutal clarity. "You were there?"

He stared at her, the shadows in his gaze deepening. "She reached out to me, but when I arrived, it was already too late. They took her, and I…"

"What?"

"I turned away."

The admission sank like a stone, the ripples of guilt radiating into the depths of her own regrets. "So you let her down."

"Not just her," he hissed, frustration igniting the fury in his voice. "I've let everyone down, including myself. I won't add another name to my list."

"We can find her," Elena declared, leaning into urgency.

He shook his head helplessly, each word coated with despair. "You don't get it. The moment you dig deeper, you will become a target too. Interests will clash, shadows will retaliate."

Elena stepped back, his words a chilling reminder of the stakes at play.

"Who do you think I am?" she challenged, clenching her jaw. "You think I don't understand danger? Do you believe I'm afraid of the truth?"

"It's not just about fear, it's about survival," he cut in, anger burning through his tone. "You have no idea how dangerous the truth is—in a world built on lies."

In the dim light of the gallery, a silence settled—a deep, resonating stillness that enveloped them as they held each other's gaze, the weight of shared pain tethering them together.

"Tell me what you know," Elena urged, but beneath the surface, her instincts warned her of the impending chaos.

The tension frayed, uncertainty shimmering in the space between them. "Meet me tomorrow—here at noon. I'll tell you everything." He stepped back, retreating from the urgency palpable in the air as the current of change swept them in different directions.

Elena watched him take a step away, her heart pounding with the realization that what lay ahead could determine their fates. Every secret unveiled was a step closer to the truth, but the culmination of betrayal hinged on the precipice, ready to spiral into chaos.

As she turned to leave, she couldn't shake the feeling that danger was closing in. The city loomed outside like a vast abyss, shadows lurking in alleys, waiting to consume her. Unveiling the secrets would unleash a flood—of truths, connections, and chaos that threatened to drown her. Yet beneath the oppressive weight lay a flicker of hope, blossoming amidst despair.

Through the challenges ahead, Elena steeled herself against the chaos, determined to confront the shards of loyalty and trust. Only time would tell how deep the betrayal ran and whether she could navigate the shadows without losing herself in their depths.

Nightshade

Into the Abyss

The rain fell in sheets, each drop drumming against the pavement like a warning. As Elena Rourke emerged from the relative safety of the neon-lit streets that buzzed with life, she was met with the oppressiveness of the city's underbelly. The ominous hint that had drawn her into this darker realm seeped into her bones like the chill of the night air. It was the type of place where shadows swallowed the innocent and secrets clung to the damp walls like lost hopes.

With every step deeper into the labyrinthian alleys, the air thickened, wrapping around her like a shroud. The scent of wet concrete mixed with a hint of decay—a potent reminder that life thrived on the fringes here, but it did so with an urgency laced in desperation. The buildings towered above her, their cracked facades and crumbling edges telling tales of former grandeur, now reduced to mere shells of their illustrious pasts.

The streetlights flickered sporadically, casting pools of light that quickly dissolved into darkness.

As Elena moved from one glimmer of illumination to the next, the sound of her footsteps echoed against the brick, a solitary heartbeat in a world that felt all too alive yet eerily dead. Each echo reverberated through her mind, drawing forth memories and fears long buried beneath her determination.

Elena paused, leaning against a cool wall, her breath hitching for just a moment. She could feel her heart racing—a dull drumbeat echoing the suspense that had begun to suffocate her. She closed her eyes, inhaling deeply, and recalled the words that had pulled her into this abyss. They had come from a source she didn't trust, yet the urgency in the hushed voice had ignited a flame of unease. "There are things beneath the surface... Look where the light doesn't reach."

She stepped back into movement, mentally plotting her course through the shifting terrain of alleys lined with graffiti and the faint glimmer of desperate eyes peeking from the shadows. The city was alive, its pulse quickening in rhythm with her own. The tantalizing allure of the vibrant nightlife was overshadowed by the grit of the underbelly, a stark contrasts where laughter was often followed by cries of despair.

If this place were a character, it would be one meticulously observed and deeply misunderstood. Elena had encountered it before, felt the seductive pull of secrets that promised to unveil truths. But as she navigated the labyrinth, she wondered about the cost of this knowledge. The shadows offered answers, but at what price?

As she journeyed deeper, the sounds became muted—the laughter and music of the nightlife fading into mere ghostly echoes.

Here, only the occasional shout between unseen adversaries and the shuffle of footsteps disturbed the stillness, a stark reminder of the danger that lay in wait. In this realm, there were no heroes, only those hiding from the light.

With each forward step, the city transformed around her, morphing from an unrelenting predator into something more sinister. It became a reflection of her fading resolve, each corner revealing a fear she'd rather ignore. Was it the potential for violence that stirred her anxiety? Or was the darkness within—remnants of her own past, whispering doubts that threatened to drag her under?

Elena stumbled slightly over a ratty piece of clothing abandoned in the gutter, but quickly caught herself at the last moment. She felt a flicker of anger rise within her—an errant emotion in a sea of uncertainty. She didn't have time for weakness. Every moment spent doubting was a moment that allowed the city to claim another soul. Her mission was clear, yet the oppressive atmosphere weighed heavily upon her, pressing down like a solid weight against her chest.

Finally, she reached an old diner, its neon sign flickering with the promise of cheap eats and sleepless nights. The windows were grimy, but a feeble light shone through, inviting her into the refuge of greasy booths and worn-out tables. The diner was filled with a mixture of faces—lost souls, people hiding amidst the bustle, some seeking shelter within the chaos, while others fell adeptly into the dark fringes, where hope was just an illusion.

Elena stepped inside, shaking off the raindrops caught in her hair, her presence drawing a few glances that quickly turned away. She walked to the counter, where a weary waitress with tired eyes and a forced smile began to draw her cup of coffee.

The ambience inside was thick with smoke and despair, yet it provided a brief respite from the outside world, a moment where time and memory could collide without judgment.

"Cup of joe?" the waitress asked, her tone indifferent.

"Looks like you've seen better days," Elena replied, her voice softer than intended.

The waitress cast a glance toward the door and leaned close, her whisper laced with caution. "You don't wanna be here if you're chasing shadows, sweetheart. Trouble rolls around here like it owns the place."

Elena's pulse quickened at the foreboding words but instead of retreating, she leaned in further. "Trouble is all I seem to find," she responded with a wry smile. "I'm looking for someone."

"Everyone's looking for someone in this city," the waitress replied as she placed the cup in front of her with a clatter. "Just be careful—some shadows like to fight back."

Elena tipped her head, grateful for the warning but too stubborn to heed it. She took a sip of her coffee, the bitter taste igniting a fire in her stomach. There was a certain comfort in its warmth, a fleeting sense of normalcy to remind her of who she was outside this world of shadows. But as she observed the other patrons—each one slowly drowning in their own sorrows—she felt the weight of her mission settle heavily in the pit of her stomach.

As she contemplated her next steps, she couldn't shake the sensation of being observed from a corner booth, the air around her suddenly electric.

She turned her head slightly, catching a glimpse of a man with deep-set eyes and a face reminiscent of worn leather. He was leaning back in the darkness, every movement deliberate, the shadows cloaking him like a veil.

Against her better judgment, Elena caught his gaze, and in that split second, she felt a connection—a pulsating current that ricocheted through the space between them. Was he an ally or another player in the symphony of deceit? She chose to ignore her instincts, focusing instead on her mission.

But curiosity nosed at her as she turned back to her coffee, feeling the weight of his stare—like a promise that things were about to become complicated.

The waitstaff bustled around her while a group of rough-looking men took over the booth across from her. Their laughter came like jagged edges, slicing through the air laden with tension. Elena couldn't help but overhear snippets of conversation, words laced with bravado and concealed violence, each syllable a thread bonding her with the darkness that stirred around her.

"Did you hear about the socialite?" one of them boomed, his voice thick with cockiness. "She's in way over her head. Poor thing won't know what hit her."

"I heard they found a few clues down by the old warehouse," another replied, his tone dripped in cynicism. "But trust me, in this city, they only lead to more questions."

Their laughter continued, an echo that wove through the oppressive atmosphere and filled the room with a vibration of inevitability.

With a sudden rush of adrenaline, Elena's attention sharpened. Their careless chatter and disruptive bravado meant that they may very well hold the very information she needed.

But how to approach them? How to navigate the dangerous terrain where shadows loitered at every corner and trust was a luxury long forgotten?

Elena set her cup down and breathed deeply, her resolve returning. She stood up, somehow finding a spark of strength amidst the questioning winds of doubt, and moved closer to their table. The room hummed with uncertainty, allowing her to navigate in the darkness like a shadow herself.

"Excuse me," she said with deliberate clarity, injecting authority into her voice.

They paused, eyes sizing her up like sharks in water, but indignation shifted into intrigue, their laughter fading into the murmur of the diner.

"I couldn't help but overhear your conversation about the socialite. I'm looking for someone—perhaps you might have answers for me."

The largest of the trio smirked, his enjoyment evident as though he thrived in this chaos. "What's in it for us, sweetheart?" He leaned closer, leering.

Elena squared her shoulders, refusing to give in to the tremor that threatened to shake her resolve. "Information is often exchanged for information. You tell me what you know, and I can make it worth your while."

His eyes glinted with arrogance. "Pretty words. But why should we trust you? You a cop? Look a little too clean for these parts."

Elena's heart raced, but her next words came smoothly, laced with an air of confidence. "I'm not asking for your trust, but trust yourself to know a good deal when it's in front of you. The socialite isn't just another lost girl. There's more at play here than the police would have you believe."

The tension shifted once more, the atmosphere thickening like tar. The men exchanged glances, weighing their options, while Elena took a seat across from them.

"I know you're in the business of information. And I'm willing to pay for the right answers," she added, determination bubbling beneath her calm facade.

"Still sounds like you don't have much to offer unless you got cash," one of the others interjected, twirling a toothpick between his fingers, smirking almost playfully.

"Why don't we make it more exciting, then?" she challenged, leaning in closer, the tension shifting into electric anticipation. "I'll match whatever you want with something you can't put a price on."

And perhaps within that very sentence dwelled the dread that had lingered at the edge of her mind. She was stepping ever so closer to danger, a precipice where she could fall and never return, but the stakes felt enormous, and she was willing to gamble.

"Interesting proposition," the large man conceded. "Let's see how this plays out."

But just as the conversation began to thaw, the diner's door swung open, drawing the chill of the night within. A figure stepped inside, silhouetted against the light—a familiar silhouette adorned in long legs and crimson lipstick. The femme fatale from their latest chance encounter had arrived, and with her presence, the room shifted once again.

Elena felt like a deer caught in headlights—a sudden rupture in her mission as the figure scanned the room. Those enchanting eyes quickly locked onto hers, sparking a connection laced with untold tension. That smile promised both pleasure and peril, calling forth the pull of unresolved longing that flickered in the back of her mind.

"Looks like the lady's got company," the leader of the trio said, amusement dancing in his eyes. "You got friends in high places, huh?"

The femme fatale was drawing closer, navigating through tables as gracefully as a dancer. Elena's heart raced—this uninvited presence brought with it an unsettling mix of desire and distrust, precariously interwoven within the very fabric of her investigation.

"Fancy meeting you here, detective," the femme fatale cooed, her voice low and sultry enough to drape over the chaos, wrapping everyone in curiosity.

Elena's mind raced, but she kept her tone steady. "I wasn't expecting company."

"Oh, but in this city, the unexpected is always anticipated." She leaned casually on the bar and allowed her gaze to linger over the trio. "And I see you've found some friends. How charming."

Elena took a quick breath, the air thickening further, engulfing her in the inescapable reality that trust was now a game of survival. Her instincts screamed at her to tread carefully, to disentangle herself from the escalating tension that vibrated in the air, ready to snap.

But choice now belonged to a desperate gamble, adjusting the odds of trust in the game. Shadows danced around them, and light once verminous in illumination turned to the perfect against dark truths lurking on the edges. She needed to escape—remaining here could very well lead to her undoing.

"Can we speak later?" she asked the femme fatale, her voice firm even as her heart raced with indecision. She didn't want to risk anything—both her mission and her soul could be lost in the chaos that unfolded.

The femme fatale's eyes gleamed with mischief as she smirked. "Maybe later means something entirely different in this city. Unraveling threads often leads to unexpected surprises, wouldn't you agree?"

As the air vibrated with tension, Elena stared into her captivating depths, willing herself to find clarity amidst the chaos. The trio roared with laughter, the dissonance snapping every fraction of her resolve, propelling her beyond the crumbling streets.

"I need to go," Elena stated sharply, pushing her chair back with urgency as she shoved bills across the table, leaving a taste of finality hanging like fog in the air.

"Don't go yet. We were just getting to the good part," the leader called after her, laced with amusement but tinged with a threat.

Elena caught the femme fatale's eye one last time before she turned to escape, the wrap of shadows falling around her as she stepped back into the night. The ominous hint had lured her into the darkness, but it was now a battleground of trust and unravelling layers, riddled with decisions that each dovetailed into deepening unpredictability.

Exited from the refuge of light and warmth, Elena embraced the night once more, her mind ablaze with whispered secrets and cornered alliances. Each shadow whispered of danger still dancing on the periphery of her consciousness, wrapping around her thoughts like fingerprints of fate.

What lay ahead was uncertain, yet the city had become a mirror of her increasingly tumultuous mind. As she plunged further into the abyss, her feet carried her forward without certainty. What she grasped now was that the darkness held the answers, but only if she was willing to confront her own fears along the way.

Confrontations

The city pulsed with a nervous energy, the comforting hum of life replaced by an underlying tension that crackled in the air like static before a storm. The streets glistened with rain, reflecting the kaleidoscope of neon signs that fought vainly against the approaching darkness. Elena stood at the mouth of a narrow alley, her heart racing as she prepared to confront the shadows that had dogged her every step since the moment she delved into the mystery of the missing socialite. She could feel the weight of the night bearing down upon her—a cloak woven from the secrets and lies of the city that threatened to suffocate her.

She had built a fragile network of leads and informants, but tonight it was all on the line. The alley loomed ominously before her, its darkness hinting at danger. The persistent rain masked the steady rhythm of her breath, steadying her resolve. Her instincts tingled; the kind of instinct that pushed her forward when every fiber of her being screamed to retreat. Elena tightened her grip on the small revolver nestled in her coat, a comforting presence against the chaos that awaited her within-

Elena stepped into the alley, each footfall echoing in the narrow passageway, reverberating with anticipation. She crossed her arms tightly, drawing her jacket closer around her as the chill seeped into her bones. The air was thick, stifled not just by humidity but by the secrets hovering just beyond her reach. Shadows flickered at the corners of her vision, but she pressed forward, the flimsy spotlight of her flashlight cutting through the murky darkness.

Voices reached her ears, low and conspiratorial, threading through her thoughts with an unsettling familiarity. They belonged to the very adversaries she sought to confront—those who wove through the city's underbelly, manipulating events for their gain, leaving bodies in their wake. Fear constricted around her heart, but rage was a fire that blazed fiercely within.

She rounded the corner, the voices coalescing into a discernible dialogue. Her pulse quickened as she drew closer, focusing on the silhouettes gathered at the end of the alley. The figures shifted like phantoms against the brick walls, and Elena squinted, desperately trying to discern their identities.

"You think she can make it out alive? You're all fools," one voice sliced through the mist like a blade, sharp and disdainful.

The speaker's laughter echoed amid a chorus of raucous guffaws that made Elena's skin crawl.

"She's already here, isn't she?" another voice replied, deep and gravelly, resonating with a sense of authority that demanded attention. "We're wasting time. Whether we bury her or let her go doesn't matter. It's too late for that."

A wave of adrenaline surged through Elena as she recognized the cadence of the man's voice. Eric Voss. A washed-up politician cloaked in power and notoriety. He thrived in the filth of this city, using its darkest corners to shield his malevolence. Her body instinctively tensed as memories flickered—conversations, accusations, and the gnawing dread that had followed her since they crossed paths.

"Shut up. She knows too much," another voice chimed in, slightly muffled by the shadows. "This isn't just about the socialite anymore. She's digging deeper. That idiocy will get her killed."

The shadows shifted, and Elena caught sight of their silhouettes—a small gathering, leaning against the grimy walls with a self-assured arrogance. Time seemed to distort in that moment, a mere fraction of reality where her choices danced upon the edge of catastrophe. She took a deep breath, blending into the cloak of darkness, a hunter poised to take down her unsuspecting prey.

Mustering what little courage remained, she stepped into their field of vision, the beam of her flashlight piercing through the gloom. "So this is where the real deal happens? Amongst the refuse of the city?" Her voice rang out, steady and defiant, cutting through their collective surprise.

Eric whipped around, his features contorting as he squinted into the harsh light. "Rourke! You shouldn't be here!" he barked, but there was a wavering edge to his tone that hinted at both fear and intent.

"Is that why you wanted me out of it? Because you knew I'd end up finding everything that lead to you?" Elena retorted, refusing to yield to the paralyzing fear that surfaced each time she faced him. Her footfall echoed, commanding authority as she stepped further into the alley, each stride a testament to her resolve.

Voss' eyes darted toward his cohorts, a silent communion, and in that moment, she perceived the cracks in their facade of confidence. The monster was angry, the bureaucrat's arrogance threatening to overtake his common sense. "You should understand that some webs are better left unspun, Ms. Rourke," he warned, venom lacing his words, his predatory gaze never leaving her.

Elena lifted her chin, a fierce flame igniting in her chest. "And you should understand that webs can easily unravel—a truth you've kept hidden for far too long."

As if released from the grip of silence, their hesitant chuckles morphed into openness, revealing the growing tension in the air. Though fear knotted in her stomach, she drew strength from a well of memories—the faces of those lost to Voss' corruption, the ones who depended on her to illuminate their truth. A thrilling sense of urgency bubbled beneath the surface. She wouldn't back down now.

"Let's cut to the chase, Voss," she said slowly, measuring her words. "You know why I'm here. I've come too far, dug too deep. Let's talk about Jessica—what you're hiding. Let's talk about the connections that go beyond just a simple disappearance."

A dull, heavy silence fell as Voss surveyed his men, a moment suspended in trepidation. They fell into an uneasy rhythm, exchanging glances—the silent calculus of understanding revealing that her presence had disrupted the expected course of their conversation.

"I think it's time you left, Rourke," Voss hissed, his voice affronted, tinged with desperation. "This is no place for you." He shifted his stance, suddenly defensive as he stepped closer, beneath the harsh yellow light glowing above them, illuminating the sweat beading on his forehead.

"Too late for warnings, don't you think?" Elena replied, as tenacity swelled within her. "Your days of hiding behind that façade are over. You can't deny the darkness you tread; your grip on this city is slipping."

With an impatient motion, Eric's cohorts tensed beside him—two men, each broad-shouldered with faces etched in cruelty. They stepped forward, ready to challenge her resolve.

"Think you're clever playing the hero, Rourke?" one of them sneered, posturing with an easy confidence, discarding any pretense of diplomacy. "This isn't a storybook. Think we won't wipe the floor with you?"

Elena's heart raced, the instinct of flight surging, but it was quickly quelled by sheer defiance. She would not let them intimidate her; she would not allow them to drown her in their darkness.

"Let's see if you're really all talk," she shot back, her words harsh and cutting. "I may be alone, but you'll find me far more formidable than expected."

"Sure about that?" Voss barked, the shift in his demeanor unmistakable as he transformed from casual control into desperate aggression. "You've got no backup here—no allies to call! You're nothing but a nuisance!"

The weight of confrontation fell heavy upon them, igniting the dangerous air around her. Adrenaline coursed through her, elevating her senses. Each of her muscles coiled tightly, ready for whatever aimless chaos might follow.

With a swift motion, the goon lunged—his bulk barreling toward her belatedly, eyes vacant with fury, driven only by the threat she posed. But Elena's mind raced quicker, deeply embedded instincts firing into action like clockwork. She sidestepped just in time, the momentum of his body carrying him past in a graceless tumble, crashing into an array of refuse, glass, and trash bags.

Another accolade of laughter erupted from Eric and the others, but Elena didn't pause. Instinctively, she pivoted—her flashlight swinging in an arc, deflecting off the grimy alley walls. Her focus sharpened as a swift kick sent her assailant sprawling back onto the ground.

"I've faced worse than you, Voss. You may control the narrative, but I will shift the tide," she threatened, pulling her revolver free from its sheath, placing it firmly upon the inward curve of her palm. The cold metal felt reassuring; it was a weight she relished against the whirlwind of fear surging within her.

In an instant, the mood shifted again. Unease rippled through the small crowd, with eyes flickering between her and their leader.

Eric stepped forward, torn. "You think you can shoot us? End this charade with a mere bullet? That's the coward's way."

"Cowardice is all you know," Elena countered, her voice steady and unwavering. "You can't stand behind your lies anymore, Voss. I will expose your depravity—campaigning and secrets intermingled with blood."

Eric's brow furrowed, confusion mingling with anger as if a mask had slipped away, exposing the true terror beneath.

Without warning, the second goon, emboldened by his partner's unexpected failure, lunged again. Time decelerated as she ducked beneath the swing of his fist, breath leaving her as she braced herself. Actions became instinctual—the role of predator and prey flipped as she forced him back, wrestling against his weight, her free hand catching his collar.

With sheer grit, they tumbled against the rain-slicked ground, splatter building an unintentional palette around them. Elena gritted her teeth, the dampness mixing with her skin, infusing her with a raw severity that paralleled the darkness of the moment. She rolled aside, drawing her revolver again, but not before he clawed at her wrist, their struggle weighted with desperation.

Suddenly, the alley seemed to erupt—a riotous mixture of grunts and slams enveloping her senses as Voss' voice rang out, distorted with disbelief. "Get rid of her! She's nothing!" In the fractal of realization and fury, she fought back harder than before, igniting a new resolve to unearth the truth buried beneath their sordid games.

Breathless, Elena found strength in the recollections of others—lost lives, distant cries for help.

Beneath the surface of the struggle lay an urgency she could not ignore. With each push, she pictured Jessica's smile; the promise of revealing the layers of darkness that shrouded her fate.

Roaring back to her feet, she focused on her adversary, but Eric and the other goon were now converging, panic spilling between their ranks as the darkness gnawed away at their confidence. "You're making a mistake, Rourke! You should've known—" he spat venomously.

But Elena wouldn't listen. She aimed, the revolver steadying in her grip, her heart pounding as concentration pinned her in place. "And you should've thought twice about crossing me," she warned, each word punctuating the silence that momentarily enveloped them.

A flicker of hesitance crossed Voss' face, the mask cracking entirely as realization dawned—a heavyweight warning that she wasn't merely a fragile investigator, but a gladiator empowered by resolute tenacity.

"Enough of this charade! You want her back? Then follow the trail!" she shouted fiercely, inching forward, yet careful to maintain her ground.

The second goon shifted, gauging the seriousness of her stare. Hesitation danced behind Eric's cold eyes—uncomfortably aware that the city's fabric could unravel in the adjacent storm. He opened his mouth to formulate a retort, but instead, the words dissolved into a silence heavy with an unexpected tension.

As he and his men stepped back into the shadows, Elena would ultimately emerge from this encounter, knowing that her pursuit wasn't simply for justice; it was an awakening, an unraveled mask revealing not only the depths of their depravity but also the culmination of her own fears transformed into courage.

With a clenched jaw, she stood in their wake, adrenaline lingering in her veins, while the shadows threatened to envelop her, daring her to resign into the depths of despair. But she tightened her grip and held the revolver firmly; this was only the beginning, and the dance with darkness had only just begun. Every confrontation wove a thread in the fabric of her resolve, an evolution she now bore, threading through each layer of pain, unlocking the power simmering beneath her skin and propelling her forward in a quest far deeper than the missing socialite—this was her reckoning.

Reflections and Regrets

Elena sank into the worn leather chair, the fraying edges whispering of countless conversations and secrets shared in this very room. The dim light cast long shadows across the walls, creating a hazy dreamscape that mirrored her turmoil. As she cradled a glass of bourbon between her fingers, the amber liquid swirled like the maze of thoughts ricocheting inside her mind. Tonight, she had a rare moment of quiet—no looming threats, no pressure of burning questions, just the soft lilt of the jazz record playing in the background.

But quiet never lasted long for her.

Every sip brought with it the sharp bite of memory, and as the warmth spread through her veins, her thoughts wandered unfettered into the depths of her past.

It felt as if she were swimming in a pool of regrets, each stroke dragging her deeper into a history she could not escape. She shut her eyes, the weight of her decision pressing down on her like a leaden blanket.

Her thoughts drifted back to the beginning of the case — the moment she had first met the missing socialite's sister, a woman whose broken voice had echoed the family's desperation. The urgency in her tone had stirred something within Elena, igniting a fire that now felt like ashes in her chest. Why had she allowed herself to be swept up in that whirlwind? The allure of truth had been intoxicating, but now it swirled around her like smoke, obscuring clarity and hope. The truth often did that. It ensnared you in a labyrinth of choices, each corners unfamiliar and perilous.

In pursuit of justice, Elena had risked everything—her relationships, her safety, her very sense of self. She thought of Marco, her closest confidant, whose unwavering support had begun to feel like a noose tightening around her neck. She could still see the hurt in his eyes the last time they spoke, incredulous at her reckless determination.

"Why do you have to do this, Elena? Why can't you just walk away?"

At the time, she had laughed it off, dismissing his concerns as mere worry. She had assured him that each step forward was a step closer to finding the truth. But as the shadows lengthened around her, even she struggled to differentiate between the truth she sought and the desire for vindication that clouded her judgment.

She couldn't shake the nagging thought that she was pursuing a ghost. The missing woman, whose vibrant life had once eclipsed so many of the city's inhabitants, had vanished into thin air, leaving nothing behind but whispers and half-truths.

Elena took another sip of bourbon, the liquid fire igniting memories from her own past—regrets that seemed to weep alongside her in the dim light. Her mind drifted to Anna, her childhood friend, a soul lost to addiction and despair. Elena had fought for Anna, believed she could save her. But in trying to pull her friend from the darkness, she had overlooked her own needs, her own safety, their relationship crumbling under the weight of unfulfilled promises. How could she have been so blind?

These reflections opened a deep wound that throbbed with guilt. She had made choices, yes, but they had brought her here, to this juncture of recovery and confrontation with her own failures. If she could have only reclaimed Anna's trust, perhaps the beauty of that friendship could have withstood the test of time. The city held no penitence for the tangled lives of those within—neither did she.

The flickering candlelight brought the room to life, dancing whimsically against the stark walls. Flashes of memories resurfaced, haunting yet familiar. The faces of the fallen flickered in her mind's eye, Anna's being paramount. Couldn't she have pulled her out of the abyss with a little more tenacity? Her willpower, tested by the rigors of her own life, seemed innocuous compared to the intensity of trying to save someone from drowning in their own existence.

Elena sighed deeply, her breath almost shuddering with the weight of emotional burden. Regrets crowded her thoughts like dark shadows, pulsating against her as if threatening to consume her whole.

Every gamble she had taken—every drop of conviction she had poured into this case and the people surrounding it—had cost her at least a part of her own identity.

Was it too late to reclaim who she once was? Navigating through the underbelly of the city had changed her, implanted scars deep beneath her skin, echoed in the cracked mirrors of her soul. What had been a thrilling game of chase became a burden, transforming her approach from passionate pursuit to a desperate attempt to outrun herself.

Yet, she had moments of hope; fleeting fragments emerged, glimmering like shards of glass catching the light when she least expected it. Her conversations with the artist had been particularly haunting; each interaction peeled back the layers of her heart she had long since closed off. His artistic expressions resonated with her own pain, and through the language of art, brief glimpses of release unfolded. As the colors spilled across his canvases, they mirrored the cascading emotions within her, a reflection of her own entrenched struggle.

Still, even within those moments of connection, shadows lurked—reminders of her failures. She could almost hear Anna's voice, sometimes echoing in her mind as if she was reaching for something solid. The brilliance of their friendship once flickered like the candle between her fingers, warmth intertwined with the comfort of shared dreams. If only she had been there, truly there, even when she should have been.

Hours passed, the jazz music weaving through the tapestry of her reflections, while her thoughts tiptoed around the edges of truth. The weight of her choices bore down heavily, each ripple of regret deepening.

What did it mean to find the truth while losing pieces of your soul in the process? In her relentless quest, she had painted herself into a corner, each brushstroke layered with confusion. The city felt like a canvas, chaotic yet familiar, and she was a mere artist grappling with undefined strokes.

Could her past mistakes lead her to enlightenment? Or had they merely sealed her fate in a tragic cycle? If the answer remained elusive, her own identity would fray, unraveling into a forgotten tapestry woven with shadows.

Elena leaned back, closing her eyes, allowing the music to wash over her like a balm. She needed to reclaim her narrative amidst the cacophony of betrayal and chaos that oozed from every corner of her existence. Identifying her vulnerabilities felt like stripping away the layers of armor she had so desperately clung to, yet it had to be done. Embracing her own flaws meant lifting the veil of deception that surrounded not only the people she brushed against but the woman she had become.

Her mind danced back to the hotel lounge where she first encountered the femme fatale. Their evening together was tinged with an unmistakable blend of allure and danger. The tension that crackled in the air had jerked at her instincts, drawing her close and yet pushing her away. Could she trust this woman, who seamlessly embodied the essence of betrayal, or was she simply reflecting the fragments of her own life?

Every conversation held double meanings, layered with ambiguity and hesitation. Had she misread those moments, processing desire against the backdrop of professional obligation?

The complex emotions intertwined, distorting her perception and wrapping her in a haze of questions. These tangled feelings—could they lead to clarity or only deeper confusion?

As dawn crept softly into the room, illuminating her thoughts, opportunities for resolution lay scattered around her like unfinished canvases. In seeking to understand others, perhaps she could unlock the doors to her own heart—facing her own pain, regrets, and the facade she had built. The truth felt like a distant echo, but perhaps it could be grasped if she took the time to listen.

Rising from the chair, she felt the stirrings of determination igniting within her once more. It was time to confront those specters, to lay bare her vulnerabilities toe-to-toe with the spectral remnants of each relationship that had shaped her journey. With every painful turn of her reflection, the path to redemption began to weave itself, stitching together a fragmented identity.

Elena stepped toward the window, allowing the morning light to wash over her, illuminating each shadow that had long since coiled around her heart. Steeling herself, she set forth anew. Each footstep should lead her closer to understanding, reclaiming not just the identity of a private investigator but the essence of the woman within—the tangled lives, the pain, all threaded together like beautiful yet chaotic artworks on a canvas waiting to be revealed.

In the city waking to light, the echoes of her past still hung in the air, but it was through those echoes she would find her strength—an exploration that would bind her to the very truth she sought.

The jazz faded into silence, yet the music of her past continued to play, each note a whisper guiding her forward.

For the choices Elena had made formed not just a reflection of her life but the very essence of who she was and who she could become.

Revelations Through the Veil

Drawing the Curtain

Elena stood before her cluttered desk, the soft glow of the desk lamp illuminating the myriad photographs, newspaper clippings, and old case files that covered the surface. Each piece felt like a fragment of a puzzle, swirling in the maelstrom of her thoughts. The once-linear paths she had traversed had grown convoluted, twisting together like the dark alleys of the city she called home. As the shadows of dusk deepened outside her window, the urgency of her investigation—now more critical than ever—pressed heavily upon her.

She inhaled sharply, dipping her fingers into a mess of papers, feeling the soft crinkle of every photograph and that, more than just a simple reminder of a life once vibrant, bore testament to a missing woman's whispers of despair. All she had were these remnants, deeply tied to a haunting case that was morphing before her eyes.

Elena could feel the electric pulse of anticipation dance within her. With each return to the material evidence of the case—evidence that now seemed to weave their own narratives—fresh threads began to emerge, forming connections that had initially eluded her. How did they all tie into the missing socialite? The question tore through her mind like a wild wind.

Among the scattered files was a picture of the socialite, her smile radiant, a live wire of luminescence captured under vibrant lights. But behind that smile lay a depth of secrets so subtle they wouldn't fall harshly from her lips. Elena felt an ache of empathy as she studied the still image—it wasn't just a person lost, it was a web woven of dreams, ambitions, and an inevitable betrayal that led to the present shadow of her absence.

With renewed determination, Elena flipped through each photo, matching them against scribbled notes of conversations held in smoky bars and glittering lounges. She recalled the femme fatale whose seductive charm had momentarily diverted her focus, yet also revealed promises of invaluable insights. That meeting had been a revelation buried in layers, offering glimpses into the socialite's life that had sparked an eagerness she fought to understand.

Her mind raced back to those fleeting words—the femme fatale's cryptic references to the missing woman's entanglements with powerful figures and hidden desires that pulsed through the very elite circles Elena was now immersed in. Each observation was a thread waiting to be tugged on, a knot inviting the tension to unravel. The connections began to blur together, straining against her understanding yet beckoning her deeper.

Shifting her focus to a stack of notes, she scanned for any phrases that hinted at deeper meanings. Words leaped from the page: jealousy, power, and betrayal. Elena sighed, feeling the weight of each term seep into her bones. There was an awful symmetry in how every lead mirrored the dark undertones that marked her city—houses of cards built precariously high, only to be blown away by the slightest breath of truth.

She leaned against her desk, the pang in her chest urging her to push through the weight of betrayal that hung perpetually in the air around her. The very alleyways she navigated in search of answers were now lined with shadowy figures, each carrying their own brand of deception, their own stories of loyalty toppled by desire.

Her gaze flickered back to the socialite's photograph, and she felt a spartan resolve settle within her. Elena wrapped her fingers around a relevant scrap of paper—the name of the corrupt politician who had tentatively crossed her path. His charm was a mask that barely concealed the insidious motives underneath. Every phrase he spoke dripped in profound mistrust, clawing at the edges of her intuition. With him, the lines had blurred far too quickly.

The stakes were rising, and it was evident that the civilization of lies Elena was entrenched in could shatter the moment secrets deemed too fragile for the world met the unforgiving winds of exposure. Elena's mind was a tangled forest; emotion unfurled in tandem with pressing realities she could barely catch a glimpse of, hidden by the fog of impression.

Still, the thought of betrayal lurked, a specter she could not shake. Every name she wrote down, every face she scrutinized—all were masks concealing intentions so wretched she found herself yearning for a single ally in this tumultuous world.

Elena hoisted herself from the desk and turned her attention toward the old corkboard on the far wall. A web of red string twisted in chaotic patterns, stringing together faces and addresses through an intricate artistry born from desperation. Color-coded notes detailed conversations and encounters, woven seamlessly into the fabric of the investigation. It was time to map out a clearer picture, to draw the curtain on the obstacles veiling her vision.

With purpose, she began plucking at the threads one by one, assigning color-coded pins to the notes she had garnered from various informants. Each revelation felt like a bolt of lightning striking a kaleidoscope.

"How does it all fit?" she murmured, barely above a whisper, as she shifted details around.

Verifying the names—filling in the gaps—the revelation of where every line of betrayal converged. Thoughts pushed into clarity as she donned the mantle of a ruthless architect, constructing a narrative where dark intentions owed to their very existence.

The evening deepened, and the air muted into a more profound darkness, laced with anticipation. She felt caffeine-fueled energy flow through her veins as she pieced together each revelation, determining which connections led her further into the labyrinth that swirled around her case.

Amid the fitful twisting shadows cast by the desk lamp, Elena's brow knitted with determination. Something had changed in the atmosphere—a crackling tension fueled her senses, ushering a whisper of truth lurking in the cracks of her memory. The missing socialite—but, more importantly, what lay beneath her disappearance—loomed just out of reach.

She picked up the photograph of the socialite once again and examined it closely. That golden smile masked something darker; it felt as though the universe was urging her to peel back the layers, to dig deeper where only shadows met her gaze. The face before her no longer bore merely an aura of allure; it murmured secrets longing to be released.

Caught in the act, she stared at the photograph, diving deep into the unseen. An unexplored layer—the thought struck her sharply; had she ever truly understood the extent of the socialite's connections? Had those secrets once been addressed as granted? Were the clues threaded together in a design mimicking betrayal soaked deeply into the fabric of trust?

Could the prominent families whose portraits graced elegant parlors be far more intertwined than she realized? Could each graceful movement across the galas and political soirées hide shadows of evil lurking behind grand façades?

Elena retrieved a notebook filled with hastily jotted notes from a dusty side drawer. It was a makeshift journal from her visits to those high-profile social gatherings where she'd rubbed shoulders with the city's elite. A field not just filled with glitz and glamour, but riddled with betrayals that ran thicker in blood than the cocktails spilled over crystal glasses.

The names she witnessed danced upon the pages—members of powerful families connected to the corrupt politician she had uncomfortably met.

"Lied to my face," she breathed, feeling the threads of trust knot tightly within her throat. Her intuition pricked at her—had she overlooked their ties? Traces that led back to the socialite?

It was not just about the present; it was a spiral through a woven past, carefully constructed over years of compromise coated in secrecy. What darkness had they protected in the prismatic brilliance of their lives?

As her heart raced, she flipped through the unevenly written notes taken at the back of each party, where conversation stirred like smoke from the tips of a cigar.

Names flickered in her mind: Murray, Tastillo, more affluent patrons entangled in a mesh she had steered away from, characteristics dancing at the edges of paranoia but too enticing to dismiss. Elena closed her eyes, allowing herself to hear the whispers that tethered the missing socialite to the audacity of the elite. The piecing together birthed depth; the air was electric, and it buoyed her courage.

She had to confront the shadow of betrayal head-on, but with whose backing?

The flicking light caught the edges of the pages, igniting all the veiled whispers that trailed right behind the missing woman. Patterns formed more tightly than she ever anticipated, reflecting truths that had lurked behind smiles and politeness, revealing the skeletons hidden in their closets—timid phantoms echoing for resolution.

The moment for confrontation loomed nearer, and she could sense their anticipated fallout beg for clarity. Elena was on the brink of discovering an electrifying truth—one that could just underscore not only the missing socialite's fate but her own sense of justice.

With resolve, she gathered her notes and sprinted toward the door, pulse racing with a conviction she hadn't felt before. The pitiless city awaited her next move, the neon lights casting long shadows that reached up to seize her spirit.

Every revelation she gathered added weight. Each facet of knowledge brought her closer to the bone of a story woven in tragedy and ambition—bold threads pregnant with desire, betrayal, loyalty, and ruin. It was about to unravel, and she would be the connoisseur standing before its unveiling.

As she stepped into the cool night air, a grin tugged at the corners of her lips. Each detail hinged on her knowledge, upon a tapestry constructed by countless missteps. The dark hand of fate was destined for confrontation, and her heart beat a rhythm of anticipation, interspersed with whispers that echoed the fabric of the city around her.

Elena navigated through the night; every person she passed could potentially be a keeper of grave secrets, a shield masquerading clever lies. Yet doubt began to mix with her determination. What paths would she still have to cross before the curtain finally lifted? Which players would step from the shadows before the final act?

With purpose and resolve, she slipped away through the fabricated lanes of the city, knowing the final curtain was nearer than she first believed.

The Calm Before the Storm

The air was thick with an almost electrifying tension as Elena Rourke stood by the window of her sparsely furnished office, watching the city breathe outside. Dusk began to settle over the skyline, casting long shadows that stretched like gnarled fingers across the cracked pavement below. Neon signs flickered to life, battling the deepening twilight with promises of nightlife, ambition, and, in some cases, treachery.

Each pulse of light was a reminder of the chaotic world swirling around her, a world she had been thrown into headfirst in her pursuit of the truth behind the missing socialite, a truth as elusive as smoke.

As she leaned against the cool glass, feeling the vibrations of honking cars and distant laughter truncating the silence, her mind danced between fleeting moments of clarity and swirling chaos. The echoes of conversations she had had—the whispered secrets in dark bars, the seductive allure of the femme fatale—washed over her like a film, blurring the edges of her thoughts. Each moment felt fleeting yet profound, illuminating the complexity of her journey. Just this morning, she'd been filled with resolve, intent on stripping bare the web of lies surrounding her case. Now she found herself floating, suspended in the uncertainty, questions spilling into her mind like water from a broken dam.

The city felt alive, alive with all its hidden truths, but each revelation stung like venom. Elena's heart raced as she took a deep breath, grounding herself against the subtle yet gripping fear that threatened to consume her. What if the truths she sought held more than she was prepared to bear? What if her relentless pursuit led her to a reckoning that demanded sacrifices she wasn't willing to make?

The gentle whoosh of the ventilator provided a mechanical counterpoint to her ruminations. With each exhale, she closed her eyes momentarily, allowing the darkness behind her eyelids to consume the chaos. In this void, she could explore the contours of her fear—a fear not just of failure but of becoming ensnared in the very fabric of betrayal she sought to untangle. Each moment of stillness, however brief, acted as an anchor in the storm of emotions crashing against her consciousness.

Her thoughts veered to the recent conversations, every fragment of information digging deeper into her psyche. The bartender's stories of late-night escapades, the femme fatale's sultry tales woven with half-truths, and the whispers from the gala—all seemed to conjoin into a symphony of deceit. She could almost hear them as a cacophony, filling the voids of her past, adding layers to the ache coiling in her chest. It was a relentless rhythm that tapped at her resolve, urging her to either dance to its tune or succumb completely.

Amid this turmoil, she felt a sudden impulse to pen down her thoughts. It was a habit she'd taken up long before she became a private investigator—a way to ground herself, to mold the shapeless tendrils of confusion into something tangible. Sitting at her cluttered desk, under the soft light of a flickering lamp, she opened her notebook, its pages filled with scribbles that mirrored her tumultuous thoughts. Lines of messy handwriting formed a chorus of her inner dialogues, ripe with contradictions and desires as raw as the wounds she'd experienced.

"What is truth?" she wrote, almost questioning herself as she scratched the pen against the paper. "Is it a shining beacon that guides, or is it merely a weapon used to cut deep and bleed?"

The weight of that realization pressed against her chest. Truth was slippery, always a few steps ahead, disguised in shadows and cloaked behind smiles. Her investigations had thrived on uncovering the hidden—a skill she had honed over years, but as she now delved deeper, the very nature of her pursuit felt like it had turned upon her. Each clue she unearthed only compounded her confusion—mixing love with betrayal, loyalty with treachery. What was she truly seeking? Was it justice for the missing socialite, or redemption for her own experiences with loss and disappointment?

Fingers pausing mid-flight, the stark contrast of doubt settled in. Her past reverberated with emotionally charged memories of failed relationships and the friends who had betrayed her trust—not unlike the very people she was investigating now. As her pen scratched across the page, she felt a sliver of recognition—a connection between her personal history and the cases she took on, drawing her nearer to the center of her internal storm.

In that moment, clarity pierced the fog. It wasn't merely the case that haunted her; it was the unresolved pieces of her own life—her inability to untangle love from loyalty, passion from deceit. She felt like a walking contradiction, a seeker of truth embroiled in a web of subjective realities. With every layer she peeled back, she could feel the implications tightening around her throat, whispering suggestions of self-doubt and guilt, of what it meant to navigate through shades of gray.

The wind outside picked up, rattling the loose window panes, and she lifted her gaze to stare out at the rampant city that had birthed her turmoil. As she watched a couple retreat into the warmth of a nearby café, the sight stirred something deep within her—an ache for normalcy, a world away from the shadows that suffocated her. She wondered what it'd be like to live without the constant pressure of secrets or the gnawing need for validation through her work. Yet, intertwined with this longing was an equally powerful realization: she couldn't abandon this pursuit. The relentless search for truth had become as much a part of her identity as the scars that lined her heart.

Elena flipped to a fresh page, her pen skimming across the paper with newfound determination.

"What do I gain from searching for the truth?" she mused, her thoughts bubbling forth. "Will clarity free me, or will it ensnare me deeper in these shadows?"

No answers came, only more questions. The city outside mirrored that uncertainty, a kaleidoscope of possibilities awaiting her yet wrapped in the unknown. Each answer she uncovered about the disappearance of the socialite felt like a piece of a larger puzzle, one she feared was designed to entrap rather than liberate.

The air hummed thickly as Elena pushed her pen down harder, the ink spilling like emotions that struggled to escape her mind. She had chased answers relentlessly, but tonight, she was confronted by the consequence of those pursuits—the choices she had yet to make regarding her own future. Voices, both those in her mind and echoing from the city's heartbeat, urged her to action; but action toward what? The impending storm loomed like a dark cloud on the horizon, pregnant with thunderous revelations.

She dared to imagine what she might find when the storm finally broke, and the calm, oppressive silence would give way to chaos. Would she emerge unscathed, or would she be swept away, consumed by the choices of others and her own misguided desires? The thought lingered, gnawing at her resolve even as she sought clarity. The complexity of the human experience unfolded before her like a dark rose, stunning but with thorns that pierced through her attempts at understanding.

The pen stopped moving again, and Elena placed it down, allowing the weight of the silence to settle. Here she was, a solitary figure in a city filled with noise, trapped in the dichotomy of her feelings. Desire versus fear. Resolution versus trepidation.

The understanding that each path she could take branched into unknown territories where truth could be as deadly as it was liberating.

At that moment, a sudden realization coursed through her—that the calm before the storm was not just an absence of turmoil but an opportunity for introspection. Emotions should not be silenced; they were to be embraced, not just the joyous flickers of hope but also the shadows of doubt. Elena breathed deeply as the silence wrapped around her, pondering the moments she had chosen to run from fear throughout her life, each time fleeing from the path of truth.

Taking another deep breath, she picked up her pen, this time letting it move freely, guided by raw emotion. "I am more than my fears. I am the seeker of shadows, a collector of truths, both light and dark, united under the guise of choice. Confrontation lies ahead, but so does revelation—and perhaps beauty, depending on what I am willing to embrace."

The page filled with her reflections, words spilling onto the paper as dust motes danced in the fading light around her. The monster that had lurked in the background—doubt, shame, guilt—began to unravel as she confronted it head-on, interpreting her fear not as a foe but as a shadow seeking acknowledgment. With every sentence, the calm washed over her, a silent promise that whatever lay ahead in the storm, she would face it not as a victim but as an active participant in her narrative.

With a final flourish of her pen, she signed her thoughts and closed the notebook, the calm that had flooded her feeling as rich as the connections she sought to forge with the chaotic world outside.

This decision—a determination to chase the truth, to embrace what it meant for her life—settled over her like a warm cloak, giving her a sense of strength even amid uncertainty. She believed in the power of her quest, knowing deep down that facing the storm head-on was the only way to unveil the secrets hidden amidst the chaos.

Elena gathered her belongings with a newfound vigor; her mind was no longer a storm of doubts. Instead, it thrummed with the resonance of her revelations. The night awaited her, filled with secrets that begged to be unearthed, and she would be the one to unveil their hidden truths. The shadows may be deep, but she was ready, ready to step into the twilight and embrace the chaos that lay ahead, prepared to confront whatever lay behind the veil.

The Final Encounter

The rain had started softly, a murmur against the pavement, but now it hammered down in ferocious sheets, transforming the city into a landscape painted in shades of gray, wrapped in a shroud of misery. Elena Rourke stood at the entrance of the dilapidated warehouse, her pulse drumming in sync with the thunder that rumbled overhead. Every instinct screamed at her to retreat, to turn away from the shadows that roiled within, yet the weight of unfinished business urged her forward.

In her years as a private investigator, she had stared down danger in its myriad forms, peeling back layers of deceit to reveal truths hidden beneath. But this time felt different—an electric tension hung in the air, heightening her senses and setting her teeth on edge. The stakes had never been higher, and the final confrontation loomed like an insurmountable wall before her.

Fingers trembling slightly, she clutched the cold metal of her flashlight, the beam piercing through the darkness as she stepped inside. The stench of damp concrete mingled with something more sinister—a lurking apprehension that clung to the corners of every shadow. She pressed on, deeper into the labyrinth, her mind racing as the memories of her investigation danced at the forefront of her thoughts.

The missing socialite, the tangled relationships, the web of betrayal… it all led to this moment, this very warehouse where echoes of the past would meet the present in a violent clash.

With each cautious step, she recalled the faces that had played pivotal roles in her journey—the femme fatale who had pulled her in with a dangerous allure, the corrupt politician whose charm belied a dark personality, and the tortured artist whose insights had cut through her defenses. All pieces of a grotesque puzzle, they had led her to this precipice of revelation.

"Elena," a voice rasped from the shadows, slicing through the enveloping silence. Her heart raced. She wasn't alone anymore. "You shouldn't have come here."

The figure emerged, a stark silhouette framed against the flickering light, and she felt her breath hitch. It was him—the politician, every bit as charming and diabolical as she remembered. He was the puppet master of ulterior motives, and his presence brought back a swell of frustration mixed with fear. How much did he know? She could already sense his power, swirling around him like a tempest, and it made her skin crawl.

"What do you want?" Elena steadied her voice, though it faltered slightly, the confidence she tried to project shaken by the reality of this confrontation. "Why did you bring me here?"

With a devil-may-care smile, he stepped closer, his demeanor slick, polished like the veneer of a man who had spent years masking his sins with charm. "You know, dear Elena, you've caused quite a stir in our little circle. Those missing pieces in your investigation? They could unravel everything I've worked for."

A pang of indignation swelled within her, igniting the anger she had buried beneath layers of confusion and dread. "You think you can intimidate me into backing off? That I'll let you continue your games while people suffer?"

He laughed softly, a cruel sound that echoed in the cavernous space. "This isn't about intimidation, my dear. It's about survival. Yours and everyone else's. Nathan never should have entangled himself with you, and Carter—"

"Carter?" The name hung in the air, twisting her stomach. Suddenly, it all fell into place; the artist, the thread that linked them all. "What are you talking about?"

"Didn't he tell you?" He leaned closer, his breath warm against her cheek. "That boy was deeper in our world than you realize. His art, his struggles—he was a tool, much like you."

Seething anger churned in her chest, battling against the fear that gripped her. "You think I'm an unwitting pawn? I've fought for every piece of information, every shard of truth. I'm not here by chance."

"Ah, but you have been roaming in the dark, Elena." He stepped back, drumming his fingers along a rusted pipe, his casual façade masking calculated movements. "Have you considered what you'll lose if you continue this path? There are fates worse than death, you know."

The air around them thickened, pressing against her like a weighted shroud. "I won't stop," she declared, her resolve hardening as shards of memory flared; the warm glow of camaraderie with Nathan, the sharp contrast of betrayal from those she had trusted. "Not for you, not for anyone who preys on the vulnerable."

The smile slipped from his face, replaced by something darker. "Then you leave me no choice, Elena. I tried to be reasonable." A low laugh bubbled from his throat. "But you must understand: in this game, there are no rules—only survivors."

Without warning, he lunged, the shadows flaring and swallowing him whole. Elena reacted instinctively, her training kicking in as she dodged to the side. A sharp crash rang out, and pain shot through her shoulder as she collided with a forgotten stack of crates, tumbling to the floor. The gritty ground scraped against her skin, and she hissed through clenched teeth as adrenaline clawed at her nerves.

"Foolish!" he spat, appearing at the edge of her vision, disheveled but undeterred. "You think you can escape? This isn't a story where the hero wins."

Wiping blood from her lip, she locked eyes with him, refusing to show fear. "You underestimate me, and I won't stand down."

"Then let's see how well you fight in the dark," he growled, kicking over another crate. Wooden splinters scattered across the floor, obscuring the narrow path that wound between shadows.

Darting forward, she weaved through the debris, pushing past the cacophony of noise. With each breath she took, the space echoed back her fears, her misgivings. But this was her moment. The chaos of the storm outside paled in comparison to the turmoil building within.

"Where is she?" Elena shouted, her voice rising with desperation as she stumbled across the floor, her flashlight flicking from corner to corner, hunting for signs of life—the missing socialite, the nerve center of all this madness.

"Who? The puppet? The trophy?" He sidestepped, continuing to taunt her with dangerous ease, his voice lacing the air with a sickening sense of control. "You think you can save her? You should be worried about saving yourself."

Elena lunged at him, fists raised, a scream of rage spiraling from her throat. But he was quicker, anticipating her movements like a predator stalking its prey. He countered her blow with a swift kick, sending her sprawling backward onto the cold concrete.

Laughter echoed in her ears, but defiance ignited within her; it would not end like this. She pushed through the pain, rising unsteadily as fury coursed through her veins. Every fleeting second, every choice made had led her into this fight, this moment of reckoning.

"Enough!" She roared, summoning the last of her strength as she charged forward again. This time, determination fueled her, and the memories of everyone who had suffered in silence became her shield.

As the two figures clashed, the warehouse morphed into a battleground, the echoes of their struggle merging with the storm raging outside. She could feel the electricity between them, a maelstrom of instinct and reaction.

An impressive kick—her foot connected with his midriff, and he stumbled back, an unforeseen surprise sparking in his eyes. She could taste the tide turning; sweat mingled with the rain that continued to lash at the crumbling walls, but she deflected the impact of uncertainty with every feint and jab.

"You think you can hurt me?" He gasped, regaining his footing, his features twisted in anger. "I've survived far worse than you. I am the storm."

"No," she shot back, gathering her air, seeing the desperation reflect in his gaze. "You only think you control the storm, but you'll soon learn that the tide can turn."

With renewed vigor, she seized the moment, launching into a flurry of strikes. Each movement was fluid, honed from her endless training, as she landed punch after punch. She felt every blow resonate, her heart racing as the energy between them surged.

And then there it was—the moment. *Crack!*

His foot slipped on shattered glass, a mirror thrown into chaos, and as he stumbled back, Elena saw it—just for an instant—the flicker of uncertainty in his eyes, unveiling the monster beneath the façade.

"Is this how you want it to end?" he taunted, trying to mask the fear creeping into his voice, though his bravado was fracturing like the glass around him.

"Yes," she answered, fierceness sculpted in every muscle. "This is how you'll be remembered."

In one last surge fueled by months of pain and resilience, she engaged him one final time, the fight escalating into a fiercely primal dance among shadows. Momentum built, and in the closing exchange, she caught him by surprise—a critical uppercut followed by an unexpected jab to the ribs. He stumbled back, surprise etched across his face as the weight of realization set in.

"Enough games!" she shouted, summoning every ounce of strength before delivering a final blow—a righteous punch driven by desperate resolution. He fell against the wall with a sickening thud, sliding down to a motionless heap on the floor.

Breathing heavily, she took a step back, the adrenaline surging in her veins as victory surged within her like an all-encompassing glow. Yet the battle had not completely unfurled, for the darkness loomed still—an invader in her world of light.

"Where is she, you monster?"

The remnants of his confidence crumbled as he lay there, momentarily stunned. "You…you won't win.

She's gone, and your attempts to save her are futile," he stammered, clearly shaken, but the malicious glint in his eyes hadn't completely faded.

"Tell me!" Elena pressed, horror bubbling inside her, pushing her toward the edge of desperation.

"She's not what you think," he gasped, the cockiness breaking further into trepidation as her threat lingered palpably in the air.

"Tell me!"

"Alright, alright," he spat, drawing in shaky breaths as if the fight had drained the life from his body. "You want the truth? She was a pawn in a game. Just like you."

Elena's heart sank, heavy under the weight of his words. A pawn? In this miserable scheme of deceit, had she truly misread everything? "What do you mean?"

"She played her part well—hidden in plain sight. I manipulated her just as I did with you, leading you away from the truth." He chuckled darkly, a hollow sound that rattled her resolve. "It's about power, about who survives when the storm breaks."

Realization hit her hard as if a glass of icy water had splashed against her face, chilling her bones. Had Carter known? Had he—

"No!" The denial erupted from her throat, raw and filled with anguish. "You're lying!"

"Am I?" He grinned, even through the pain. "That's the game. It never ends. If you want to save her, you'll have to dive deeper into the very darkness you shun."

The echo of his words lingered as they echoed back through her mind—a chilling entrapment bending her perspective until the shadows pulsed with life.

With grinding resolve, she moved toward him, fueled by desperation—and rage. "What did you do?"

But he laughed, a sound devoid of humanity. "You can't grasp the tragedy of it all, can you? You are just another shadow among the many, and when the time comes, you will understand what darkness truly means."

"No," she affirmed, fists shaking at her sides, her heart threatening to burst against the pressures of truth. "I will not be a pawn. Not now, not ever."

He pursued a gaze toward the door, conscious of impending defeat. "You're just a kid, Elena. A girl trapped in a game that has no mercy."

"You underestimated me," she breathed, her voice farmore resolute now, ignited with a fierce determination. "And I will expose every morsel of your deception."

With a final glance at his crumpled form, she turned and sprinted toward the door, the air crisp as shadows enveloped her. She felt each moment surge around her, urgency propelling her into the night where the echoes of thunder mirrored the pulse of her heartbeat.

The storm had unleashed its fury, and in those fleeting hours, she had fought—unknowingly—against the very essence of her fears. Only knowing now that the final encounter was not just about the confrontation, but the subsequent battle inside her mind—a soul wrestling against the weight of darkness honing in around her.

Yet she could feel it—rebirth simmered under her skin, igniting the dawn of newfound hope, though it still flickered cautiously in the shadows of uncertainty. The remnants of adrenaline coursed through her, but she was no longer afraid.

As the door swung shut behind her, the storm raged on outside, but beneath it all, she could hear the fragile whisper of trust being reborn, tracing a path toward the secrets that awaited her next move.

The Hour of Reckoning

The Storm Unleashed

The sky had darkened into an oppressive canvas of charcoal clouds, brewing with wrath as if it, too, were aware of the storm tearing through the lives of the city's inhabitants. Thunder rumbled overhead, announcing an impending downpour, while jagged flashes of lightning illuminated the streets momentarily before plunging them back into shadow. The air was thick with electricity, a palpable tension that seemed to coil and twist around Elena Rourke as she stood at the edge of chaos, unbound by the stillness that preceded the storm.

Elena moved through the slick streets, each step echoing her mounting anxiety. Rain began to fall in heavy sheets, drenching her as wind whipped around, throwing her thoughts into turmoil. Each droplet that hit her skin felt like the weight of unresolved questions, the ache of betrayal, and the pulse of danger that had become a constant companion. She was on the brink of an abyss, teetering between her desperate quest for truth and the haunting shadows of her past.

As she rounded the corner of an alley, a harsh cough erupted from the darkness—followed by frantic whispers and the shuffle of footsteps. Instantly, her pulse quickened. The storm outside mirrored an internal tempest, amplifying her senses while drowning out the remaining echoes of hope she had clung to. She stepped closer, clinging to the wet brick wall, her flashlight flickering weakly as she squinted into the gloom.

The silhouetted figures emerged, huddled beneath an awning, their faces obscured by the downpour. The flickering of light revealed the tension in their stances, the way their bodies leaned towards each other, as if sharing secrets that could bring destruction. Just then, a voice broke through the pouring rain, sharp and trembling, resonating with an urgency that made her instincts flare. "They found out. It's—it's all going to unravel!"

Elena's heart raced. She crouched behind a dumpster, her breath shallow as she eavesdropped, desperate for details that could connect her scattered pieces of an intricate puzzle. The storm wove chaos into the fabric of the night, and in that moment, she became acutely aware that she was venturing deeper into a web strung with deceit and danger, all in pursuit of the missing socialite.

"Just keep your mouth shut," another voice barked, this one gravelly and authoritative. "We can't afford any loose ends. Not now. Not when we're close. Do you understand?"

The underbelly of the city resonated with secrets, its very foundation trembling in the wake of fading loyalties and fractured alliances. Elena could feel the beat of her heart pounding against her ribs, a reflection of the storm raging within her as well as without. She was weaving her way through shadows, seeking allies where trust had become an elusive concept.

Suddenly, one of the figures stepped forward. A flash of lightning illuminated his features—a familiar visage, twisted in desperation. It was Marcus, a low-level informant who had initially tipped her off about the socialite's disappearance. He had always danced on the edge of danger, and Elena had been drawn to his volatile energy. Now, that energy crackled with trepidation.

"Look, I don't—" he began, but was silenced by a fierce grip on his collar. The authoritative figure loomed over him, a malevolent force that squeezed the breath from the room.

"I said no loose ends. You know what that means. If you don't want to end up like her, keep your mouth shut."

Elena inhaled sharply, the instinct to intervene raging against her better judgment. She pressed closer, acutely aware that her presence remained unseen amid the torrent of rain. She watched as Marcus flinched, fear suffusing his features as he nodded, his voice barely above a whisper. "I won't say anything, I swear…"

Another bolt of lightning struck nearby, illuminating the gravity of the moment. Elena recognized this as the crux of the storm—not merely outside, but within her own heart. Tensions soared, pushing her closer to the edge of revelation, though the price of that discovery threatened to be her very life.

In that instant, the chaotic rumble of thunder transformed into a growl that mirrored her increasing anxiety. She had to make a choice. She could no longer be an observer. With her hands trembling against the clammy bricks, she ducked into the alley, each step more deliberate than the last.

"Marcus!" she called out, her voice cutting against the torrential roar of rain, igniting a spark of chaos. His eyes widened—fear and surprise colliding—before they flickered towards the figures who now turned their attention away from him.

"Who's there?" the authoritative figure barked, a deep frown carving his face as he raised a dim pistol directed at Elena's direction.

"Stop!" she commanded, unwavering even as the weapon glinted in the sporadic glow of the lightning. "I'm not here to hurt anyone. I just want to talk."

Marcus stood frozen, caught in the crossfire of surprise and apprehension, his expression shifting from relief to dread. The other figure advanced, his grin sinister under a veil of rain, showcasing teeth like daggers. "You've made a grievous mistake stepping into this mess, lady."

Elena's heart raced, aware that the storm was escalating both outside and within.

The tension wound tighter, each second suffocating her with the weight of fate—a reckoning she had both anticipated and dreaded. Her pulse synced with the torrential downpour, feeding the chaos that consumed her surroundings.

But in the glare of desperation, something inside her ignited. "You think you can silence me? You're wrong. I know what happened to the socialite. I know about the lies, the corruption that you're all a part of!" Her voice rang out defiantly, a battle cry amidst the storm.

"Enough!" he thundered, taking a step closer, his eyes glinting like shards of ice. His grip tightened on the weapon, anger igniting the air around them, electric and volatile. Lightning cracked again, illuminating the alleyway into stark relief, and Elena seized that moment.

In a heartbeat, she lunged to the side as the gun fired—a deafening roar that pierced through the chaos of rain and thunder. The shot ricocheted off the brick wall, a deafening explosion against the torrential backdrop. Time slowed; the air thickened with tension, a blend of fear and determination overpowering her senses as adrenaline surged through her veins.

"Run!" Marcus shouted, sensing the moment's urgency as he too made a break for freedom. But Elena stood firm, her resolve hardening, ignited by a deep-seated need to confront the truths buried beneath the shadows that engulfed her. She would not be another victim lost in the chaos; she would unveil the narrative built on mistrust and manipulation.

"Stop!" she yelled, forcing herself to focus through the cacophony—the rain hammering against her skin—the storm's wrath closing in.

A chase ensued, a symphony of chaos conducted in the heart of the storm. The colors of the world blurred, shapes and shadows melted together as she sprinted down slick streets, feet pounding against the cobblestone as panic chased them through the deluge. Each breath she took tasted of adrenaline, each heartbeat resonating with the clamor of the storm above.

Marcus ducked around the corner, his coat heavy with rain as he veered into the darkness of an adjoining alley, but Elena couldn't seem to shake the feeling that danger was closer than she dared let on. The shadows of the night stretched longer as if specters of the past were clawing for release, sharing the same air with her as she chased the truth.

Before she could decide her next move, a fierce body slammed into her side, sending her sprawling onto the wet pavement. The hard surface knocked the breath from her lungs as she flailed beneath the weight of her assailant, struggling to push the weight off. Rain mingled with the slick cobblestones, refracting the city's fractured lights into streams of color swirling in a puddle beneath her.

"Who sent you?" the figure growled, overwhelming her with his presence—a storm of intimidation laced with desperation that trapped her in a vice of fear. Her eyes widened, struggling to register his intentions as she grappled to pull free.

"Let me go!" she gasped, the urgency clawing at her throat.

"Answer the question," he spat, gripping her shoulder tighter, igniting the fire within her to fight back.

She felt her own resolve rising in defiance, harkening back to the truths she had uncovered—the people united by deception, darker than the shadows that flanked them.

With a surge of strength, she twisted and kicked, her foot connecting with the man's knee—a calculated strike that knocked him off balance. She seized the opportunity, scrambling to her feet, but the grip of the storm above shook the very ground beneath her resolve as she planted herself into a defensive stance.

"You're foolish to come here alone, Rourke," he snarled, his face illuminated for a heartbeat in the glow of another flash of lightning. It was then that she recognized him—it was the corrupt politician she had sought to expose, his ambitions entwined with the dark fate of the socialite that had drawn her into this labyrinth of intrigue.

"Elena!" Marcus shouted from the shadows, but she barely had a moment's reprieve. The rain poured in torrents, the entire world swallowed by roiling clouds as she felt the crushing weight of fate pounding down like the drops drenching her.

"Can't you see, Senator?" she shot back, her voice rising above the storm. "People are going to find out the truth. You can't conceal it forever!" Despite her pounding heart, she found strength in her assertion, a fire ignited by all she had lost and for all she hoped to save.

"Do you think I fear threats from a little investigator?" he mocked, eyes gleaming with malice. The sound of thunder clapped overhead, a cruel reminder that storms bring destruction to all in their path. "You have no idea what you're playing with. You think you're the hunter, but you're merely the prey."

And with that, he lunged forward, an act of desperation and aggression colliding in a cacophony of light and dark. She twisted to evade him, the rain obscuring her vision as she plunged into a side street that led deeper into the heart of the chaos.

"Come back, Elena!" Marcus's voice pierced the kaboom of thunder. "It's not safe out there!"

Fate had become entangled with every heartbeat. Each echo of his plea thrummed through her veins as strands of her essence merged with the storm—her doubts, her pain, her drive to uncover the truth merged into one pivotal moment.

Elena stumbled around yet another corner, legs burning with exertion, rain blinding her as she pressed forward. The streets were alive, alive with shadowy figures emerging through the downpour, warped dancers in the chaos she had unwittingly joined.

She sought refuge in a narrow archway leading into an abandoned courtyard—the weather-lashed edges of the city consuming her as she held her breath. Surely, she could find escape from the storm, if only temporarily, before the reckoning collided with her entire trajectory. The darkness enveloped her, a cocoon against the chaos outside.

Yet just as the impulse to breathe faltered, sounds swelled around her—a murmur of shuffling feet, shifting weight, and the unmistakable click of firearms. The storm intensified, pounding down with ferocity threatening to drown out her thoughts, but Elena steeled herself, knowing the answers she sought lay just beyond this veil of chaos.

"It's over, Elena!" came the shout from behind, the senator's voice thundered as he broke through into the courtyard, his silhouette barely visible under the torrent. "You can't hide from the inevitable."

"Maybe not," she spat back, heart thudding in her chest as she gripped tightly onto the jagged edge of hope, desperately pulling in breaths infused with adrenaline. "But I will face it head-on." Her mind raced through options, the threads of fate intertwining with revelations she had fought to unearth. She would not be penned into anyone's narrative but her own.

Lightning flashed again, illuminating a broken statue—ephemeral reminder of beauty lost to time. They were audience to the impending chaos, embodying the weight of history's lessons against those who failed to learn from them.

"Where's the socialite, Senator?" she yelled, the thrum of the storm invigorating her as she pressed deeper into uncertainty. "What have you done to her?!"

He hesitated, fury darkening his features as the rain streamed down his face, washing away the veneer of respectability he clung to. "You really think you can stop what's already in motion?"

"Like hell I can't!" Her heart thundered as she adopted a battle-ready stance, refusing to back down. "This storm is bigger than you realize."

Just as she felt the tide of emotions surge, she heard a voice pierce through the chaos—a softer echo against the clamor of rain, trembling yet resolute. "Elena!" It was Marcus again, pushing his way through the tumult, eyes wide and pleading. "You have to leave while you can!"

Elena's gaze darted between the senator and Marcus, tension tightening like a snare in her chest. "No! We'll figure this out together. We can't just walk away." The reckoning was here, and no storm would deter her from the truths she had fought tooth and nail to reveal.

"Stand back!" Marcus yelled as if sensing the culmination of chaos entering a realm beyond control. "We need to go, Elena! Now!"

"No! Not until the truth comes out!" Hot determination wove itself into her words, intensifying the storm's rage as thunder crackled above, making shadows dance with the ferocity of their confrontation; this was a moment of bloom and unraveling.

The senator hurled forward, rage bubbling beneath layers of control as he lunged toward her, purposefully closing the distance meant to intimidate. In that split second, time unraveled—the city around them radiating with tension as questions of life and death collided. There was no room for fear or hesitation.

Elena braced herself, her body harmonizing with the storm, the wind lifting the hair from her face, urging her toward the heart of the storm.

"Get down!" Marcus shouted again, expression a mask of fury as he charged beside her, an unexpected ally against the tide of treachery.

But the senator was too quick, moving as a tempest unto itself. With a formidable roar of violence and control, he raised his weapon.

As the bullet soared through the night, images of her loved ones danced in her mind's eye—a flash of memories wrapped in love, pain, and hope. In her gut tightened an awareness of stakes intertwined taller than skyscrapers, more complicated than the web of the city itself.

A panic surged as she ducked, the shot echoing behind her, and another gasp punctured the darkness—a cry blossoming into thorns as anguish infiltrated the storm.

The world twisted again—it was a moment of raw catastrophe, chaos breaking as thunder shook the ground beneath her; rain cascading as Elena fell, as bodies collided in a morass of desperation.

In that instant, time stretched infinitely as her mission collided with passion. The storm unleashed its tempest, and so did she.

Choices Under Fire

Elena stood at the precipice of chaos, the storm raging around her as the city erupted in a cacophony of voices and sirens. The air thick with tension and the smell of rain, she felt the weight of the world pressing on her shoulders, an unbearable load she had carried for far too long. She was no longer just a spectator in this tangled web of deceit; she had become a pivotal player, entangled in a deadly game where every choice carried the potential for both redemption and ruin.

The confrontation had spiraled out of control, igniting a firestorm of emotions that crackled with pent-up energy.

Shadows danced erratically in the dimly lit alley as the neon signs from the surrounding buildings flickered ominously, casting a surreal glow on the faces of those caught in the turmoil. Elena's heart raced as she glanced at the figures around her, each one betraying a multitude of intentions beneath their facades. Friendship, loyalty, ambition—these fragile threads intertwined and strained, threatening to snap at any moment.

Her pulse quickened, echoing the chaos outside. Memories of her friends' laughter, the warmth of trust and camaraderie, flooded her mind, but they felt like ghosts now; echoes of happiness swallowed by the darkness that surrounded her. The hard choices she faced loomed like specters in her mind, demanding her undivided attention. In the eye of the storm, clarity could be as elusive as the fleeting moment of stillness before the skies unleashed their fury.

"Trust is a dangerous game," she whispered to herself, recalling the warnings she had dismissed in her quest for truth. Desire, that insatiable hunger that propelled her forward, had now left her vulnerable and exposed. A chilling realization settled within her — every ally could be a potential adversary, and every decision could shift the course of her life.

Elena's breath quickened as she turned, her gaze settling on the source of the turmoil. A figure emerged from the shadows, a familiar silhouette that sent a rush of conflicting emotions coursing through her veins. It was Marcus, her closest confidant, standing at the intersection of loyalty and betrayal. His expression was unreadable, but there was a tempest beneath the surface, a silent war raging within him that mirrored her own inner chaos.

"Marcus," she called out, forcing her voice to steady despite the turmoil. "What's happening? We need to make a choice!"

He stepped closer, eyes dark with concern, but their shared history hung between them like a fragile thread, barely holding. "Elena, we're out of time. They're closing in. We either fight, or we run."

Those words landed heavily, resonating deep within her, echoing the choice she had dreaded facing. The fight or flight instinct surged to the forefront of her mind, but she felt the deep-rooted desire to protect the people she loved, the friends who had become family, and the fragile bond she shared with Marcus. How could she abandon everyone now, after everything?

Elena struggled with the weight of it all, the crushing reality of her situation. Her journey had begun with questions, with a simple desire to uncover the truth of the missing socialite, yet it had led her into a labyrinth of intrigue where loyalty had become a tainted concept. Now, diving deeper into the murky waters of deception, she could feel the impending loss looming ever closer.

"Do we have a plan?" she asked, conscious of the gnawing doubt creeping in. She had always been driven by ambition—a desire to seek out the truth, no matter the cost—but at this moment, she found herself questioning whether that ambition had blinded her to the very real dangers surrounding her.

Marcus hesitated, glancing over his shoulder as the sounds of footsteps echoed ominously through the alley. "There are things I haven't told you, things that could change everything," he admitted, his voice low and tense.

Questions flooded her mind, but fear had stolen her voice.

Whatever he was about to say could either help her reclaim her footing in this collapsing world or send her spiraling into the abyss. "Then tell me now, Marcus. We're running out of time!"

He took a step closer, his voice barely above a whisper, but it was laced with urgency. "It's connected to the socialite. We aren't just looking for her; we're in the middle of a much bigger game. One that's been playing out long before we even stepped foot into this mess. And it leads to..." His words trailed off into the heavy silence of the alley, the weight of unspoken truths pressing upon them.

Elena's heart thudded painfully in her chest, each beat a reminder of the love and ambition that had driven her to this point. "Leads to what, Marcus? We can't afford to hold back now."

A flicker of uncertainty crossed his face as if he waged a silent war with himself. "It leads to the politician. They plan to use the missing woman as leverage, and if we don't act now, everything will unravel."

Her breath hitched at the revelation — a chilling realization that widened the chasm of betrayal that loomed between them. The politician she had encountered, their dangerous game shrouded in sophistication and charm, had drawn them deeper into the fray. How many layers of deception had she missed?

Suddenly, the pieces began to form a distorted picture, converging into the web of lies that enveloped her. Decisions loomed before her, each carrying repercussions that would ripple into the lives of those she cared for.

"Do we trust him?" she asked, her voice thick with emotion as uncertainty swirled in her gut. "After everything he's done, can we?"

Marcus looked conflicted, his gaze flickering away as if searching for an answer in the shadows. "We don't have a choice. We have to play his game. It's the only way to find the socialite and expose the truth."

The thought of embracing yet another layer of deception gnawed at her conscience, yet the alternative seemed darker still. To walk away now would be to surrender, to abandon those whose lives hung precariously in the balance.

"So we go in knowing we might be pawns in his game?" she questioned, her pulse quickening.

"Pawns can become queens if played correctly," he replied, and in that moment, Elena felt an echo of their camaraderie resurge between them—one that brought with it a fleeting sense of hope. But had their shared ambitions clouded their judgment?

With the footsteps growing louder, Elena felt the urgency sharpen her instincts. "Then let's do it. We'll confront him on our terms." But even as she said it, doubt lingered in the back of her mind.

Every choice sculpted from ambition, desperation, and desire wrestled for dominance over her heart. With each moment, she understood the line separating right from wrong was fading, morphing into a gray haze where loyalty drowned in betrayal.

As she steadied herself for the confrontation ahead, she felt the familiar stirrings of determination rise within her. She would become the architect of her fate, refusing to allow anyone to dictate her choices. After all, she had made it this far, defying the very odds stacked against her.

"Together?" she asked, locking eyes with Marcus, hoping for reassurance.

"Always," he replied, an unspoken pact binding them in their shared resolve. And as they moved forward, she knew every step taken brought them closer to the truth, even as the shadows closed in around them.

The universe felt heavy as they approached the businessman's opulent office. It stood like a fortress, defying the storm that raged outside while embodying the secrets caged within. With each step along the polished floor, the atmosphere grew thick with anticipation, a weight pressing against her chest. What awaited them beyond these doors would undoubtedly test their loyalty, bring to light the treachery that threatened to consume them.

As the ornate door swung open, Elena felt time slow, each second stretching out impossibly as she crossed into the lion's den. The politician sat behind a vast, mahogany desk, a facade of calm amid the chaos surrounding them. His discerning eyes met Elena's with a calculating intensity, as the shadows danced across his face, revealing a predatory nature beneath the cultured veneer.

"Ah, Elena Rourke, the ever-persistent investigator," he greeted, voice smooth as silk, the warmth of a smile failing to touch his cold eyes. "And Marcus, my loyal partner in this little enterprise."

Elena tightened her hold on her resolve, channeling her inner strength. "We need to talk," she stated, moving closer, compelled by the urgency of their situation.

"Talk? Or negotiate?" he questioned, his tone deceptively light as the weight of his intentions lurked beneath the surface. The exchange of words felt like a delicate dance, the stakes layered with unspoken tension that hung heavily in the air.

"I'm done playing your games," she declared boldly, infusing her voice with conviction. "We want the socialite back. The truth. It's time to lay everything out on the table."

A flicker of amusement crossed his features, but beneath lay a current of menace that sent a shiver down her spine. "And what makes you think I'll give you anything? You're merely pawns in this larger strategy."

The challenge lingered between them, yet Elena felt the weight of reason grounding her amid the chaos. If they couldn't dismantle the façade, if she allowed fear to dictate her fate, the innocent would continue to suffer. Lose herself to the shadows.

"We hold the cards too," she stated firmly, glancing at Marcus, mirroring their shared determination. "We won't let you use her as leverage or toy with lives for your gain."

The smile faded from his face, replaced by an intensity that churned with the fury of the storm outside. "Very well, then," he replied, his voice a low hiss. "Let us see if your ambition is enough to withstand the fallout."

As their discussion unfolded, Elena felt the stakes rise higher, the pressure eclipsing the hope that had illuminated her path. The intricacies of their choices tightened their bonds, weaving them deeper into a tale fraught with peril. Each revelation challenged her resolve and drove her further into conflicting loyalties.

As tensions flared, Elena faced the ultimate question: What was she willing to sacrifice to reclaim trust in a world filled with shadows? Love, ambition, survival—all collided in this moment where betrayal loomed like an inescapable fate. Her choices could either solidify their bonds or shatter the last remnants of her life into chaos.

"Choose wisely, Elena," the politician warned, his voice threading through the chaos, offering one last reminder of the dangers that lay ahead.

As truth and deception intertwined, she held on to hope—the flickering ember that refused to be extinguished despite the darkness closing in. Whether she emerged victorious or found herself ensnared in a web of betrayal was yet to be seen. But one thing was certain: the choices made in this very moment would echo through her life, reshaping her destiny in ways she could scarcely fathom.

Emboldened by their resolve, the storm raged on outside, a reflection of the tumult within her, the cacophony of desires clashing against the hard truth of survival. They would emerge from the fire anew or succumb to shadows that threatened to consume them whole. And as the storm broke overhead, sending rain cascading against the windows, Elena was resolved; she would choose, fight, and reclaim her destiny from the very hands of darkness.

Resolution and Consequence

The storm had passed, leaving behind a city washed clean yet still trembling from the echoes of chaos that had unfolded just hours before. Rainwater pooled in the cracks of the asphalt, glistening like tears as dawn's slanted rays broke through the leaden clouds, introducing a hesitant light to a world wrapped in shadows.

Elena Rourke stood on the balcony of her apartment, staring out into the new day, her heart racing with the remnants of adrenaline that had coursed through her veins during the tumultuous night. The events that transpired were seared into her memory, a vivid tableau of desperation, betrayal, and the flicker of hope that flickered dimly at the edge of her consciousness.

The euphoria of surviving the confrontation had been intoxicating, but now it felt hollow. What was victory when it came at such a steep cost? She felt the weight of decisions made under fire, decisions that had irrevocably altered the fabric of her life and the lives of those she touched. The cold morning air nipped at her skin, rendering her bones heavy—each breath a reminder of her current reality. Every clash of emotions fought within her, echoing off the walls of the small space that had, until now, been her sanctuary.

Elena turned back inside, pacing the confined area where sunlight dared to seep through the partially drawn curtains. The flickering bulb hanging from the ceiling provided little warmth, just like her recent interactions with the suspects and allies that had formed the complex fabric of her investigation. She reached for the coffee pot, allowing the familiar ritual to ease her tension as she watched the dark liquid swirl in the glass pot—the comfort of caffeine amidst chaos.

As the coffee brewed, she glanced around her apartment, her gaze falling on the clutter of case files and photographs strewn across her small desk. Each image bore silent witness to the drama that had unfolded—the missing socialite, the enigma of the femme fatale, the corruption nestled deep within the city's political veins. And her own reflection superimposed over it all, a constant reminder of who she had become throughout this ordeal.

She thought of the artist, whose haunted eyes revealed pieces of truth that had shattered her constructs of trust. The conversations they'd shared resonated, echoing through her mind like haunting melodies, their themes layering together in a complexity that felt both unbearable and enlightening. The bond forged through shared pain spun a web around them, ensnaring her in thoughts of their crossroads: the artist fighting against his own demons and the resolve she had found in battling her own.

The coffee pot clicked off. She poured herself a full cup, savoring the rich aroma. The steam rose, warming her face and offering a momentary respite from the chill that engulfed her. She took a sip and let the heat wash over her, igniting memories of fragile moments between life and death amidst gunfire and desperation. With every sip, she reminded herself of the choices that lay before her, choices that could mean everything and nothing at the same time.

She knew she needed to unravel the threads of betrayal woven tightly around her heart. The storm did not merely wash away the remnants of the darkness but had unveiled truths she could no longer ignore. Those who claimed to have her back had oscillated between allies and enemies, their motivations concealed behind smiles painted with deceit. The trust she had built with each of them had been tested, fractured, and in some instances, utterly broken, revealing their true selves in the aftermath of conflict.

The city outside her window began to awaken, the soft sounds of cars stirring to life like whispers in an ancient cathedral. Somewhere distant, a siren wailed, pulling her attention back to the present moment. She put down her mug and began to sort through the papers, flipping through photographs, notes, and hastily jotted reminders.

Each flick captured a fragment of her tumultuous journey—details about the socialite, the mafia connections, cryptic characters with tangled loyalties.

But today was different. Today, she would not merely collect evidence. Today, she would reckon with her own choices and the consequences they had wrought. With her mind set, she combed through the case files, seeking patterns of behavior, motivations, and past transgressions of each player involved.

As she noted the connections, names began to intertwine in her mind, whispering sinister histories that blended with the present chaos. The femme fatale, with her intoxicating allure, was more than a mere distraction; she was a catalyst in this story, a complex character with layered motivations that both repelled and attracted Elena. The hidden desires lurking beneath their exchanges were painted with the brush of regret, and the yearning for acceptance screamed within both their souls.

Then there was the artist, who had seen her in a way no one else had—the raw truth behind her façade as a tough investigator. His vulnerability echoed her own, and it was that connection that lingered in her thoughts. What did his willingness to reveal himself to her say about her? Had she used him to disentangle her own grief, or had he genuinely stirred compassion buried deep within her?

With each passing moment, the vague sense of redemption she sought shifted between her fingers like grains of sand. The depth of her regret began emerging from the fabric of recollections, intertwining with the present as she wrestled with her decisions.

The parking lot of the law firm where the corrupt politician held court lay in view from her window, a constant reminder of the systemic decay that infected the very heart of the city and the world she lived in. Elena clenched her fists, sharpening her resolve as she recalled the veiled threats the politician had delivered to her—a showdown that had left her reeling.

Facing the harsh realities altered her perception; the city was not just a collection of shadows, but a living organism, fully aware of its contradictions. Trust had always been a luxurious commodity, a glimmering mirage shimmering over the horizon—just out of reach. And yet, through the despair, she found perhaps the greatest realization: she was not alone in this journey.

Every figure that had crossed her path—from the grizzled bartender whispering tales in the smoky bar to the shimmering elites at the gala masquerading behind their gilded facades—held pieces of the puzzle. She understood their duality and, in turn, reflected on her own: a private investigator living her life in shades of gray and often drowning in the murky waters of morality.

As the sun rose higher, she found herself reaching for the phone, fingers hovering over the screen as she debated calling the one person who seemed entangled in the very fabric of this story—her former confidant who had stood by her side from the very beginning. They had shared laughter and tears and yet, there remained a rancor in the air that lingered like the scent of stale cigarettes.

But trust, fragile as it was, needed tending—to rebuild and reclaim. She exhaled a shaky breath, readying herself as she dialed the number, each ring resonating like the rhythmic beating of her heart.

"Hello?" came the familiar voice, thick with concern but lightened by an underlying layer of warmth.

"Lucy, it's me." Elena paused, taking a moment to collect her spiraling thoughts. "We need to talk… about everything."

In that moment, as they set a time to meet, Elena felt the first flicker of resolve ignite in her chest. Today would not merely be an exploration of the past, but a forging of new pathways with those who remained willing to traverse the jagged edges of their fractured trust.

The meeting was appointed for the evening, leaving the hours to stretch like an elastic band ready to snap. Intrigued by the idea of confronting the ghosts that haunted her, she took to the streets, considering the sprawling city that had birthed this chaotic symphony. Each corner was laced with memories of laughter, sorrow, and naive trust; the outlines of blurred faces etched into her mind like an artist's careless brushstrokes, begging for recognition—no, for redemption.

The deeper she wandered into the urban labyrinth, the more she noticed how interconnected lives unfolded around her—each passing figure encapsulated in breaths of their own stories. A street artist painted vibrant murals that juxtaposed the claustrophobia of unfulfilled dreams against the backdrop of the concrete jungle. Couples strolled with hands intertwined, sharing familiar glances filled with unsaid promises while others crossed paths in hurried isolation, each a testament to the myriad relationships that sparked both joy and heartache.

She returned to the bar where her investigation had taken root, the air thick with the audible energy that thrummed through the city's veins. The bartender recognized her and gestured her over—a small solace amidst swirling chaos. "You survived the night, huh?"

"Barely," she replied, trying to mask the tremors still pulsing through her body. "Seems like it's just the beginning."

The bartender poured her a drink—no frills, just something to calm her racing heart—and she took a moment to let his presence ground her. The familiarity of this place played its part, but the heaviness that beset her heart remained, filling the corners of her mind with lingering shadows.

"Have you heard anything since…"

"Word travels fast," he said, leaning closer, sincerity in his gaze. "The word is that it's not over. People are still making moves. You ought to be careful."

"I'm aware." She took a sip, digesting the implications that came with his warning. The atmosphere pulsed with deeper truths she had yet to grasp, secrets that coiled beneath the surface waiting for the merest hint of light to expose them.

"Don't let them stir fear in you. You know this city. You've cut through the darkness." His encouragement brought her courage back into alignment, a reminder that even when the night felt suffocating, she had fought to uncover slivers of light.

Saluting the bartender with a nod, Elena departed into the streets once more, piecing memories and decisions together as she returned to her apartment to prepare for the upcoming confrontation.

Hours later, just as twilight draped its silken fabric over the city, she found herself in the familiar café, where the scent of roasted coffee mingled with the cool evening breeze. She spotted Lucy seated at a table near the window, their eyes meeting in a moment filled with unsaid apologies.

"Hey," Elena greeted, the tension palpable as she took a seat across from her long-time friend and confidant.

"Hey," Lucy replied hesitantly, her voice tinged with concern. "I was worried about you."

"I know I've pushed everyone away," Elena confessed, feeling the weight settle between them like an unwelcome guest. "But I need to understand how we got here."

Lucy leaned in, her gaze steady. "We're both to blame for the distance. You've been fighting your demons on your own."

The acknowledgment stung, but it also sparked a desire within her to confront the fractured reflection they had avoided. "My decisions—were they wrong?"

"Not wrong, Elena," Lucy reassured her, her voice soothing yet firm, "but misguided. You lost sight of the bigger picture."

"Maybe I thought I could bear it alone." A torrent of emotions flooded her eyes as she recounted the grappling chaos of the investigation, layers of deception that had ensnared them both. "I thought I had to protect you. I wanted to shield you from the risk."

"Do you think I can't handle risk? You've forgotten who I am."

The passion ignited between them, a rich tapestry of scars and ambitions hanging in the air. In that moment, it became evident to Elena that the deeper layer of their friendship had always been about mutual protection; and in shielding Lucy, she had trapped herself in the silence.

The conversation meandered through their shared past, excavating wounds anew, but what emerged from the ashes of pain was a bittersweet understanding. Each recollection unveiled how trust could shift and weather storms only to rise stronger afterward, like a phoenix stirring from the ashes of betrayal.

"I can't change the past," Elena said, tracing a finger over the rim of her cup, "but I can choose how I move forward."

Lucy offered a gentle smile, acknowledgment dancing in her eyes. "We'll find a way to rebuild it together."

In that moment, the sense of resolution began to settle—a dawning recognition that her choices defined not just her own fate but also had the power to restore the bonds frayed by doubt and fear. The painful lessons lingered, carrying with them memories etched in heartbreak, but they also paved the way toward redemption. Their conversation shifted from questioning to affirming what mattered—their friendship, their resilience against the tempest that had threatened to extinguish it.

As they departed from the café, the lingering fears of mistrust remained, but a flicker of hope emerged, festering with the possibility of redemption.

The air was thick with first breaths of forgiveness—heartbeats that echoed the city's relentless pulse as Elena ventured back home, the sunrise symbolizing a burgeoning dawn, lighting her way toward the truths that lay ahead.

In the following days, she found solace in both the subtlety and distinct layers of her relationships. Each encounter with the figures she'd woven into her story became an exploration of identity against the backdrop of confrontation.

Returning to the artist's studio, she sensed the weight of memories enveloping her like a familiar blanket, shrouding her in contemplation. His canvases had evolved, reflecting the turmoil she'd witnessed in him previously. Each brushstroke felt deliberate, a struggle against chaos that mirrored her own battles.

"Your work has changed," she noted, her voice barely above a whisper.

He turned, gaze piercing through her facade, revealing himself as an observer amidst the chaos—a witness to the evolution of both their lives. "Art always evolves with the creator," he said softly. "Like we do. I heard about the confrontation."

"It wasn't easy," she admitted. "But it forced me to confront deeper truths—about you, about me."

There was a moment—a silence charged with connection. He dipped his brush into the hues of pain and promise, transforming their unspoken feelings onto the canvas before them. "How do we reconcile with our past?" he asked, seeking honesty.

"Maybe by facing the shadows that haunt us."

Their conversation dug beneath the skin of anguish, exploring how they might embrace broken pieces rather than hide from them.

"She was lost. The socialite," he mused, pausing. "In her search for identity. It resembles what you're looking for, isn't it?" Their eyes locked, understanding passed between them as raw emotions played across both their faces.

In facing their demons, Elena saw glimpses of the redemption she craved, a glimmer that spoke of the resilience they both embodied amidst the unforgiving world.

For weeks, the investigation pressed on. Secrets unraveled into a tangible web of deceit, guiding her back to the roots of their motivations. As she peeled back layers of betrayal, she felt the fragility of trust echoing throughout the vibrant streets. The city pulsed around her—no longer a collection of shadows but a mosaic of lives entwined beautifully yet chaotically.

Finally, the culmination of her efforts brought clarity and resolution to the case—an undeniable truth that echoed within her own heart. The revelations she uncovered showcased the thin vein separating justice from manipulation. With the corrupt politician's arrest and the dark underbelly of connections exposed, Elena knew it was not just a win for justice; it was a step toward reclaiming her sense of self.

As the shards of chaos settled into something more recognizable, she stood before the world, emboldened by the understanding that trust was fragile yet wielded immense power when nurtured and protected.

The connections she built were not mere threads spun out of convenience; they formed a fabric rich with stories waiting to be shared.

She began the day by returning to the café—her sanctuary—to sip her coffee among familiar faces and strangers alike. Sharing snippets of her narrative as Elena Rourke, the investigator on the mend, she painted her journey not just with the complexities of desire but with the revelations of identity that came from embracing the warmth of community and trust.

In those small yet significant moments, she felt the ache of solace seconded by the gentle reminder that every choice carries a weight, but it's the choice to rise from it—surrounded by others—that fosters connection and bolsters resilience against the tide of uncertainty. Through forgiveness, vulnerability, and facing the fractured mirrors of their past, there blossomed new beginnings steeped deeply in the fertile soil of personal growth.

And as the sun dipped below the horizon, she felt it—the palpable understanding that this journey would never really end. Not with the uncovering of truths or the resolution of betrayals. It was simply the dawn of a new chapter, layered with complexity, filled with struggle, and paved with an unyielding pursuit of trust amid shadows of deceptions. In her heart, she nurtured the courage to face whatever awaited her around the bend with wisdom gained from pain; for she had survived—and now, she was ready to thrive.

Faces of the Dark

The Choice Made

The first rays of light pierced through the cracks in the drawn curtains, casting soft, golden hues across the otherwise dim room. Elena Rourke sat on the edge of the bed, the sheets tangled around her like the thoughts spiraling in her mind. Outside, the city was awakening, a new day unfolding amid the secrets of the night that had just passed. But for Elena, dawn brought not peace, but a pivotal moment laden with consequence.

The events of the past few days played out in her mind like a film loop—each twist and turn in the investigation hanging over her like an impending storm. The relentless chase for the missing socialite had pulled her deeper into a world laced with betrayal and desire, nudging her ever closer to the edge. As she sat in the early morning light, she was aware that the choices she made now would define her future, solidifying her identity amid the shadows that once nearly consumed her.

Elena took a deep breath, the crisp air filling her lungs, and felt the weight of every decision pressing down upon her. Just days ago, trust had felt like a fragile illusion, easily shattered by the harsh truths hidden beneath polished façades. But now, with dawn breaking, trust had become her only tether to the person she yearned to be—a professional investigator capable of unraveling chaos, yet also a woman seeking connection in a world filled with darkness.

She grasped the cool metal of her necklace—a small anchor pendant resting against her chest. It had been a gift from her mother, a reminder to stay grounded amidst the turbulence of life. This same pendant carried more weight now than ever before, symbolizing not just a connection to her past, but also the decisions that would propel her into uncertain waters.

In the previous night's confrontation, Elena had come face-to-face with a dangerous truth: the political labyrinth surrounding the case, with the corrupt politician as its puppeteer, had ensnared her in a web of manipulation and deceit. She had been forced to consider who she could trust and whether the alliances she formed would protect her or lead to her ultimate downfall. As the sun's rays seamlessly danced across her skin, blending warmth and worries, the dichotomy of her choices shimmered before her, and she felt a stirring within.

Her phone buzzed next to her, pulling her from her reverie. It was a message from Garrett, her closest ally in the investigation, asking to meet one last time before they pursued their respective paths. With a swift motion, she typed a response, her fingers hovering over the screen longer than necessary as she contemplated what her message signified.

Let's meet. It's time to talk.

The words felt heavy even as she pressed send. It was a sign that she was ready to confront the reality of what their partnership had come to symbolize for both of them—a connection steeped in shared trauma and the desire for resolution. The meeting wasn't just about their investigation; it was a crossroads moment where they would both lay bare their choices and the shadows they bore.

Elena stood up and walked to the window, peering out at the awakening city. The streets glistened with fresh dew, illuminated by the rising sun, a stark contrast to the gritty alleyways that concealed the city's darkest secrets. She recalled the moments spent in those shadows—the whispers of betrayal in the smoky bars, the shallow laughter at the gala, the seductive promises from the femme fatale who had entangled her heart. Each encounter had taught her something about human desires, fears, and the lengths to which people—herself included—would go to protect what mattered most.

In the depths of her reflection, Elena caught a glimpse of her turbulent history, the relationships that had shaped her, scarred her, and allowed her to evolve into the investigator she was today. Some bonds had fallen apart in chaos, while others had deepened, forcing her to grapple with the weight of trust and the risks involved in making herself vulnerable.

With each heartbeat, she reminded herself of the choices she had made along the way, many born from desperation and yet others echoing a deep-seated need for redemption. The juxtaposition of her journey—the relentless pursuit of truth against a backdrop of hidden lies—had brought her to this singular moment, where the promise of change felt attainable yet frighteningly fragile.

As the sun climbed higher, streaks of orange and pink unfurling in the sky, she felt a resurgence of hope mingled with uncertainty. Her thoughts shifted towards a future that beckoned with possibility but also lingered with the ghosts of her past—each choice, a reflection of her own desires, tangled in the complexities of trust and loyalty.

An overwhelming need for clarity surged forth as the clock ticked away the minutes. She had worked too hard to allow fear to dictate her actions any longer. Standing tall, Elena made a choice to confront her past, to unearth the truths that lay buried beneath the surface. It was time to engage with the consequences of her decisions, whether they led her to redemption or sent her spiraling back into the darkness.

The meeting with Garrett needed to encompass more than just strategic planning for the case—it demanded honesty, vulnerability, and a shared resolution. He had been an anchor for her while caught in the raging storm, a partner who shared not just the weight of the investigation but the shadows that lurked within. The journey had tested their limits, but now, as the dawn illuminated the path ahead, she sensed the power of their connection could be the key to overcoming the chaos surrounding them.

The sun's brilliance flooded her senses as she dressed quickly, planning to meet Garrett near the docks—a location reminiscent of their first conversations—a place where hopes had mingled with uncertainty, the water serving as a mirror to their fears and desires. As she walked through the quiet streets, she felt a shift within herself, the resolve solidifying as she relived the relentless journey that had brought her here.

Elena's pulse quickened as she neared the docks, the salty breeze kicking up energy within her. She could visualize the scene, their conversation diverging into both strategic discussions and the core of their emotional bond—a complex dance of trust woven with threads of lingering affection and respect.

Garrett stood by the edge, adorned in a well-worn leather jacket, his gaze resting on the water, deep in thought. As she approached, he turned to her, eyes meeting hers with an intensity that sparked a fire in Elena's chest. The moments without spoken words hung in the air between them, fraught with unaddressed tensions and past concerns.

"Hey," he greeted, his voice low, tinged with a mix of softness and urgency.

"Hey," she replied, searching for the right words, for the emotional bridge she needed to cross between them. "Thanks for coming."

"Of course. I knew you'd want to discuss everything." A pause lingered before he continued, "This whole thing…it feels like a whirlwind, and last night…"

"Last night changed everything," she interjected, feeling both the weight of their shared experience and the revelatory nature of their recent encounter with the politician. "We can't ignore it."

"Agreed," Garrett replied, his jaw tightening as he cast his gaze back to the water. "But what does that mean for us? For the investigation?"

Elena took a steadying breath, bracing herself for the confrontation of not only their shared mission but also the emotional currents beneath. "We have to decide what we're doing moving forward. This isn't just a case anymore; it's our lives."

He turned back to her, eyes narrowing slightly, the fierceness of an investigator igniting his expression. "Are you saying we should walk away?"

"Not at all. I want to confront this—this web we've been caught in. I don't want to leave anything unsaid or undone," she stated firmly, her voice resolute. "We've become partners, Garrett, in more ways than one. We need to navigate our next steps together."

Garrett moved closer, the tension palpable in the air between them. "So, you're saying we lean into this partnership? Explore whatever this is between us?"

The question ignited a whirlwind of thoughts within her. The consequences of their partnership darted through her mind, echoes of feelings that had begun to blur the lines of their professional connection. Trust lay dangerously tangled in unspoken feelings—she could feel her heart racing, urging her onwards.

"Yes," she replied, her voice steady despite the maelstrom within. "If we're going to untangle this, we need to confront it head-on. Together, we can pierce the shroud of secrecy, but we must also confront our emotional scenes."

A flicker of recognition crossed his face, and the gravity of her statement settled in the air like fog. "Do you think we can really do that? Navigate the line between personal feelings and professional responsibility?" He took a step closer, the intensity of his presence overwhelming but undeniably comforting.

Elena nodded, absorbing his gaze, the flicker of awe and vulnerability sparking her courage. "We have to try. I feel the connection, Garrett. If there's ever going to be clarity, we must embrace the truth."

As the weight of her confession hung in the air, silence enveloped them both. The world around them receded, leaving only the two of them caught in a moment of profound understanding. In that stillness, the fragile beauty of trust shimmered like the sun rising over the water, illuminating their shared path.

Finally, Garrett spoke, his voice a low rumble. "Then let's tackle this together. Whatever comes next, let's dismantle the layers, confront what lies beneath."

With a wave of relief and warmth spreading through her heart, Elena smiled, cherishing this pivotal moment, signaling the shift in their relationship—their choices clearing a path through the labyrinth that had once eluded her. Together, they stood at the precipice, ready to challenge the shadows that had loomed for too long, guided by mutual respect and shared aspirations for truth and justice.

The sun surged higher, brighter now, its warmth enveloping them as they stepped away from the edge, their journey intertwined into the rising light. The choice Elena had made—to trust and to grow—was a testament to her journey, illuminating not just a way forward, but the strength of the connections she embraced.

As they turned away from the shimmering water, she could feel the fabric of her past weaving with her present. Together, they were not just two investigators caught in the unraveling narrative of a case; they were two souls daring to confront their emotions amid the chaos, ready to face the shadows and claim the light.

The journey was just beginning.

The Shattered Mirror

Elena stood in the quiet aftermath, gazing into the broken fragments of glass scattered across the cold floor of her small apartment. Each shard reflected the dull glow of the morning sun filtering through the tattered curtains, the light dancing on the edges as if mocking the chaotic turmoil that had just unfolded. The jagged pieces mirrored the turmoil in her heart—a heart that had weathered storms, yet felt more fragile than ever.

The night had been a tempest—an orchestra of pain and revelation that left her reeling, wrestling with choices made in a haze of desperation and defiance. Now, in the soft embrace of dawn, those events coiled within her; the weight of them settled around her shoulders like an unwelcome cloak. Memories surged forth, vivid and unrelenting, pulling her back down the shadowy corridors of her past.

She recalled her life before the investigation, a life filled with the innocence of trust and belief in the goodness of people. This belief had been her compass, guiding her through her early years, allowing her to forge connections, take chances, and open herself to others. But each experience carved deeper lines in her psyche, reminding her of a world cloaked in deception. Her childhood memories were tinged with muted colors; faded images of laughter echoed through the alleys of her mind, punctuated by the harsh reality that grew increasingly vivid with every trust betrayed.

The sudden betrayal of a childhood friend had ripped through her like a sharpened dagger—a wound that never quite healed. It had been the first time someone she trusted had shattered her perception of loyalty.

Instead of protection, she found herself standing on the precipice of heartbreak, grappling with the realization that even the people closest to her could harbor darkness within.

After that moment, the path of escape led to an armor of emotional distance. She learned to keep others at an arm's length, to shield herself behind layers of skepticism and disillusionment. The ache of loneliness was often more palatable than the pain of betrayal. The mirror of her past, now fragmented, reflected a young girl who wore sadness like an ill-fitting dress, desperately trying to fit into a world where trust had become a rare commodity.

As time ebbed, the shadows in her life thickened, blending into the fabric of her identity. She found solace in the pursuit of truth—an obsession that prompted her to become a private investigator. Each case revealed little shards of humanity, bits of lives intertwined with misery, secrets, and deceit. She sought to unveil these hidden truths, finding a sense of justice in the unraveling narratives of others. Yet, even as she fought valiantly for the stories of those who had lost their way, she couldn't shake the feeling that she was also chasing shadows of her own creation.

One case lingered longer than the rest, a haunting specter that returned to her in fleeting moments of stillness—the disappearance of the socialite. The chaos of that investigation forced her to confront not just the outer world but the inner workings of her very self. It was a cataclysm that encountered her deepest fears and regrets—flashes of moments spent questioning her choices, ruminating over past decisions that now felt heavy with consequence.

In the mind's eye, she saw the reflections of various faces—each representing a choice made, a connection forged, a trust given.

There was the femme fatale who had lured her into a captivating yet treacherous dance, every whispered story leaving a scar that cut deep. The artist, too, lingered; his tortured soul had reflected fragments of her own anguish, revealing her vulnerabilities in painful detail. Each character she had encountered had formed a part of the journey, but they also showcased the fractures within herself.

Elena knelt, as if drawn by an invisible force, and gingerly picked up the largest shard of the mirror, its edges sharp, reminding her of the glint of treachery. She ran a finger along the jagged surface, allowing the cool sensation of glass to ground her amidst memories of chaos. The image that stared back was not just her reflection but an embodiment of every piece of herself that whispered of shame and regret.

Who was she now, standing here amidst the wreckage of her choices? She had been so adamant in her pursuit of truth, yet the very quest that had once empowered her now echoed with the haunting question of whether she had sacrificed too much to achieve it.

Silence hung thick in the air, wrapping around her like a shroud. The world beyond her apartment felt distant, the noise of the city muted; even the birds outside paused as they sensed the weight of her introspection. It was the stillness before a storm—a storm that did not merely threaten the outside world but churned deep within, a tempest that begged for release.

With each breath, she recognized the need for self-forgiveness. The tumultuous decisions she had made were no longer just acts of defiance: they were choices born from a desire to not just seek the truth but to find herself, to reclaim the woman she had lost in the shuffle of shadows and deceit.

She longed to break free from this cycle of pain, to embrace the parts of her that had weathered storms and had survived, no matter how jagged and raw. With that realization, anger bloomed within her—not anger toward others but at herself, for allowing the past to hold such a powerful grip on her present. It was time to lay down the burdens she had carried, to transform that anger into something more potent, more healing.

Elena set the shard down gently, watching the way the light refracted, intertwining colors that danced and merged. In that moment, she understood that the scars were not just marks of failure; they were also testaments to survival, each one a narrative that wove into the fabric of her existence. The intricate tapestry of her life boasted not just darkness but vibrant splashes of resilience, courage, and the pursuit of truth.

Tears pooled in her eyes, a mixture of pain and revelation, and she let them flow. The journey toward acceptance began with acknowledgment. The paths taken—the ones that led her into the arms of danger, deceit, and ultimately, redemption—were all part of her story, shaping the unbreakable core of her identity.

As she wiped away the tears, she felt lighter, the shadows of regret receding slightly, the sun shining brighter on her face. She had battled demons both within and without; she had lost and gained, cried and laughed. But these experiences were not just marks of survival—they had chiseled her spirit, carved her identity into something more formidable than she knew possible.

In the quiet of her apartment, a sense of acceptance washed over her, leaving an imprint of peace where turmoil had once churned.

She rose to her feet, confronting the remnants of her past, not as a victim but as a warrior. The shards of the mirror were no longer just broken pieces; they were fragments of a whole that had endured, a reflection of a woman who had emerged from darkness.

Stepping away from the glass, she felt a new sense of clarity. The path forward lay before her, unwritten yet promising—a canvas ready for new choices, bold strokes, and, with them, the opportunity for redemption not just for herself but for those she sought to help.

A flicker of determination ignited within her. Each choice made from this moment forward would build upon the lessons learned, a foundation of growth rooted in self-forgiveness. She would no longer be defined by the shards of her past but by the strength she had summoned to stand before them. It was time for Elena Rourke to move forward, guided by a newfound conviction that even shattered mirrors could reflect beauty when placed in the light of understanding.

With the sun fully risen, she marched toward the door, her heart surging with the promise of new beginnings. The city awaited, filled with shadows and secrets, but now, Elena felt armed with an unyielding sense of self. No longer would she be merely an observer of lives entangled in darkness; she would rise as a force of change, illuminating paths for others as she carved her own truth into the fabric of the world.

New Beginnings

The pale light of dawn crept through the window of Elena's modest apartment, contrasting sharply with the tumultuous events of the previous night. The city outside, still shrouded in the remnant fog, appeared fragile, its beauty tinged with melancholy.

She sat on the edge of her unmade bed, the crisp sheets rumpled from restless hours, her mind swirling with the echoes of the choices she had made, the betrayals she had witnessed, and the scars that had healed only partially.

Elena's thoughts surged like the tide, pulling her into the depths of reflection. The last remnants of night whispered haunting memories—faces from the shadows, all dancing across her mind. Figures who had once seemed trustworthy now loomed like ghosts from a past she longed to escape. The echoes of laughter and the sharpness of confrontations intertwined, a reminder of the fragile fabric of human connection.

As she rose, the morning sun spilled across her floor, illuminating the dust motes that floated in the air like tiny stars. She moved through her apartment, a place filled with remnants of a life lived in pursuit of truth. Photos adorned the walls—snapshots of moments so vibrant yet painfully tinged with solitude. Each image was a reminder of the relationships she had forged and the trust that now felt like shards of glass scattered across her heart.

Today was different.

Today marked a turning point.

Elena poured herself a cup of strong coffee, its rich aroma intertwining with the scent of fresh air wafting through the slightly open window. She leaned against the counter, watching as the light slowly brightened the room, filling the corners with warmth. A few months ago, she had often felt like a specter in her own life, drifting from case to case, believing that every truth uncovered added another weight to her already burdened soul. But now, as she cradled the steaming cup, an unexpected flicker of hope ignited within her.

The events of the previous night had unraveled the tightly woven strands of deception that bound her to both past allies and unforeseen enemies. The confrontation she had with the corrupt politician had been fierce, a battle of wills where every word exchanged felt like a duel, exposing hidden agendas and revealing the cracks in her own trust in humanity. Yet, in that moment of chaos, she had found a sense of clarity. The truth had emerged, not just about the socialite but about herself, revealing the underlying strength that had always been there, just hidden beneath layers of doubt and expectation.

As she prepared for the day, a decision had formed in her mind—a path toward new beginnings that beckoned powerfully, urging her to step beyond the shadows that had clung to her for so long. She no longer wanted to be the victim of her circumstances, nor did she want to allow the past to dictate her future. Instead, she would weave the narrative of her life anew, deliberately, and with intention.

Armed with resolve, she dressed carefully, selecting a deep navy blouse that mirrored the morning sky, paired with tailored trousers that hinted at her growing confidence. Every piece of clothing she wore felt like armor, each stitch a promise to herself. Elena took a moment to gaze at her reflection in the mirror, reaffirming the strength she had uncovered within. There was a fierce determination in her eyes that hadn't been present before, a glint that spoke of the journey she was committed to undertaking.

Before leaving her apartment, she paused at a small framed photograph perched on her desk—an image from better days filled with laughter and dreams that seemed far away now.

It was a picture of her younger self, bright-eyed and full of ambition, standing next to her best friend, a steadfast companion who had believed in her when even she struggled to do so. The warmth of that memory pulsed through her, layered with a tinge of sorrow, but today it felt like a beacon.

"Today," she whispered to herself, "is a new beginning."

Elena stepped out into the bustling city, the sun now fully ascended, casting golden light across the streets. The energy was palpable, a rhythmic pulse that thrummed beneath her skin. People moved hurriedly, focused on their own paths, creating a mosaic of lives intersecting in the labyrinthine urban landscape. For the first time, Elena felt like an active participant rather than an outsider watching life unfold from a distance.

As she navigated through the throngs, her phone buzzed in her pocket—a message from a familiar number. It was from Mack, her closest confidant and a loyal ally in her investigative journey.

"Let's meet at The Daily Grind. I have some intel that could be crucial for you moving forward."

Elena smiled, the corners of her mouth lifting in genuine happiness. With renewed purpose, she made her way to the café, eager to absorb whatever information Mack had unearthed, but also excited to share her own revelations about the case and her plans for the future. The coffee shop buzzed with conversation, the air thick with the aroma of freshly brewed coffee and the sweet scent of pastries.

Mack was already seated at their usual corner table, the one bathed in the soft glow of morning light filtering through the window.

He looked up, a mix of concern and curiosity etched on his face as Elena approached, her energy radiating like the sun's rays spilling around them.

"Elena, you look different," he remarked, taking in her appearance with a warm smile that reassured her. "Stronger, maybe?"

"Stronger," she echoed back, the word tasting liberating on her tongue. "I've come to some realizations."

Through sips of coffee and animated dialogue, they dissected the previous night's chaos. Elena shared how she had confronted the politician, every detail spilling forth, punctuated by the freedom she felt in finally owning her narrative and pursuing her truth. Mack listened intently, nodding as she spoke.

"I knew you had it in you," he encouraged. "You've always had this resilience. Sometimes you just need to face the storm to find that strength."

"It's not just about the case anymore, Mack," Elena confessed, her voice growing earnest. "I want to rebuild my life. I want to focus on the things that matter—trust, love, and the people who genuinely care about me."

Mack leaned back in his chair, a smile breaking across his face as he encouraged her candidness. "That sounds like a plan. And trust me, you deserve it."

The conversation shifted, weaving through personal anecdotes and shared laughter as they built on the foundation of their friendship, a bond that Elena realized she had neglected for too long while losing herself in the shadows of her work.

"Speaking of trust," Mack said, his tone turning more serious, "there's a group of us looking to create a network. Private investigators, advocates... people who want to help each other out. I think you'd be a great fit."

The idea warmed her, igniting a spark of excitement within her. The thought of being part of something larger, a community committed to unraveling truths and supporting one another, resonated with her freshly kindled desire for healing and connection.

"I'd love that," she replied, the words tumbling forth, her heart buoyed by the possibilities awaiting her. "Count me in."

Hours melted away as they exchanged ideas, laughter, and dreams for the future. The world outside was bustling, but inside, Elena felt suspended in a space of promise and hope. Every word they shared stitched together a sense of belonging, a tapestry interwoven with threads of trust that she had thought were long lost.

When they parted ways, Elena stepped back into the vibrant streets, her spirit buoyed and her resolve strengthened. The day unfolded before her like a blank canvas, waiting for her to paint her path with rich hues of experience and new beginnings.

She spent the next few days diving deeper into her personal relationships, reaching out to old friends, and allowing herself to be vulnerable, to both offer and accept support.

Connections were rekindled, dining experiences enriched by laughter and stories shared over shared dishes, and her heart swelled with gratitude for the reminder of human connection.

Elena found herself returning to the artist's studio, seeking both inspiration and understanding amid the captivating chaos of color and emotion expressed through art. The last time she had visited, they had touched on fragile souls and the stories art could tell.

The artist welcomed her with a warm smile, his studio glimmering like a treasure chest filled with vibrant creations. "Elena, I've missed our conversations," he said, his voice rich with sincerity. "Your perspective always brings new life."

"Thank you," she replied, a spark of excitement flashing through her. "I've been reflecting on our discussions, and I think it may be time for me to create my own piece."

A glimmer of intrigue flickered in his eyes. "A brave undertaking. What inspires you?"

"New beginnings," she said, her voice strong. "I want to explore the fragility of trust, the beauty of relationships, and how we evolve through the challenges we face."

"Art can speak to so many depths," he replied thoughtfully, guiding her toward a blank canvas sprawled on an easel. "Let it guide you. Dive into your feelings. Let the brush dance."

Elena took a deep breath and picked up a brush, envisioning the emotions swirling within her.

The vibrant colors began to flow onto the canvas as she painted, stark shapes and shades emerging, each stroke embodying a piece of her journey—a journey filled with shadows, betrayal, love, and, ultimately, hope.

Each session in the studio brought more healing, more clarity. It became a space where she could express herself freely, a cathartic release from the past, where time stood still, allowing her to sift through her emotions.

Days melted into weeks, and soon the canvas became a vibrant reflection of her growth—a powerful tapestry of experiences that consumed her during her dark days, intertwined with radiant bursts of hope representative of her new future. As she stepped back to view the finished piece, she felt a sense of completion wash over her.

Elena had transformed the shadows into something beautiful, embracing both her scars and her light. It was in this moment she realized that while the past could never be erased, it could be reshaped into something meaningful.

As the seasons shifted, so too did her perspective. One evening, watching the vibrant hues of sunset spill across the horizon, Elena embraced the realization that her life was a myriad of beginnings. Each day held the potential for redefinition and rebirth, and she found strength in knowing that closure was not an end but a path that opened new doors.

With the glow of twilight illuminating the city, Elena made her way home, feeling the renewed pulse of life within her—a heartbeat thrumming with purpose. Every decision brought her closer to the woman she wanted to be, one who embraced her vulnerabilities and learned to dance with the shadows instead of shying away.

Elena stood before her window, gazing down at the bustling streets below. The city, once a labyrinth of uncertainty, now pulsed with possibility. She felt tethered to it, knowing she belonged to the very fabric of it all, woven with the lives, stories, and choices of others. Each thread had its significance, and each connection held the promise of growth, trust, and understanding.

In this quiet moment, Elena whispered a silent vow to herself—to continue to pursue truth, cultivate trust, and foster relationships filled with authenticity. She felt a warm smile crest her lips, the light from the setting sun bathing her in a golden glow.

This was not just an ending; it was a powerful beginning—a rebirth ignited by choices, love, and resilience. With every dawn that broke, Elena would rise and embrace each new day, ready to greet the shadows, knowing that she possessed the strength to steer through them with grace.

The shadows still existed, yes, but they no longer defined her. No longer would they dim her spirit or cloud her heart. Instead, they served as a reminder of her journey, a journey that had led her toward this moment—a moment filled with renewed hope and infinite possibilities as she stepped boldly into the light.

Thank You for Joining the Adventure!

Wow, can you believe it? We made it to the end together! First off, thank you from the bottom of my heart for embarking on this journey with me. It's been a wild ride filled with twists, turns, and a sprinkle of magic, and I truly couldn't have asked for a better companion than you. As you close this book, I hope you're left with a sense of wonder and excitement, ready to tackle your own adventures with the same spirit we've shared on these pages.

Remember, the stories we create don't just exist in books; they linger in our hearts, igniting the bravest parts of our souls. I want you to take these tales with you, let them inspire you to dream without limits, and remind you that every day is a blank page waiting for your own unique story. So go on, step out into the world and paint your life with the vibrant colors of your imagination!

I encourage you to share the magic with those around you. Talk about your favorite parts, discuss the characters that made you laugh or cry, and even create your own stories inspired by what you've read. Stories are meant to be shared, and I trust that this one will spark conversations and connections that lead to new adventures.

As we part ways for now, I hope you'll revisit the world we created together. Let it be a safe haven to escape to whenever you need a little extra magic in your life. Remember, you are capable of crafting your own tales—ones that are more fantastical and exhilarating than you can even imagine. The sky's the limit!

Until we meet again in the realms of imagination, keep shining bright. I can't wait to hear about all the adventures you're going to embark on. So, here's to infinite stories waiting to be told, and to the brave souls who dare to tell them. Let your light continue to shine brightly in this world that can sometimes feel a bit dull. You are magic; never forget that!

Yours in storytelling,

Ron Milione

ISBN:
9798282723311

Made in United States
Orlando, FL
17 May 2025